SECRET CODERS
Monsters & Modules

GENE LUEN YANG
& MIKE HOLMES

First Second
New York

"It was this wonderful time between magic and so-called rationality."
—Wally Feurzeig, co-creator of the Logo programming language, on the early days of Logo

First Second
New York

Copyright © 2018 by Humble Comics LLC

Published by First Second
First Second is an imprint of Roaring Brook Press,
a division of Holtzbrinck Publishing Holdings Limited Partnership
175 Fifth Avenue, New York, New York 10010

Library of Congress Control Number: 2017957417

Paperback ISBN: 978-1-62672-610-9
Hardcover ISBN: 978-1-62672-609-3

Our books may be purchased in bulk for promotional, educational,
or business use. Please contact your local bookseller or the Macmillan Corporate
and Premium Sales Department at (800) 221-7945 ext. 5442 or by e-mail at
MacmillanSpecialMarkets@macmillan.com.

First edition, 2018

Book design by Rob Steen

Printed in China by Toppan Leefung Printing Ltd., Dongguan City, Guangdong Province

Paperback: 10 9 8 7 6 5 4 3 2 1
Hardcover: 10 9 8 7 6 5 4 3 2 1

Chapter

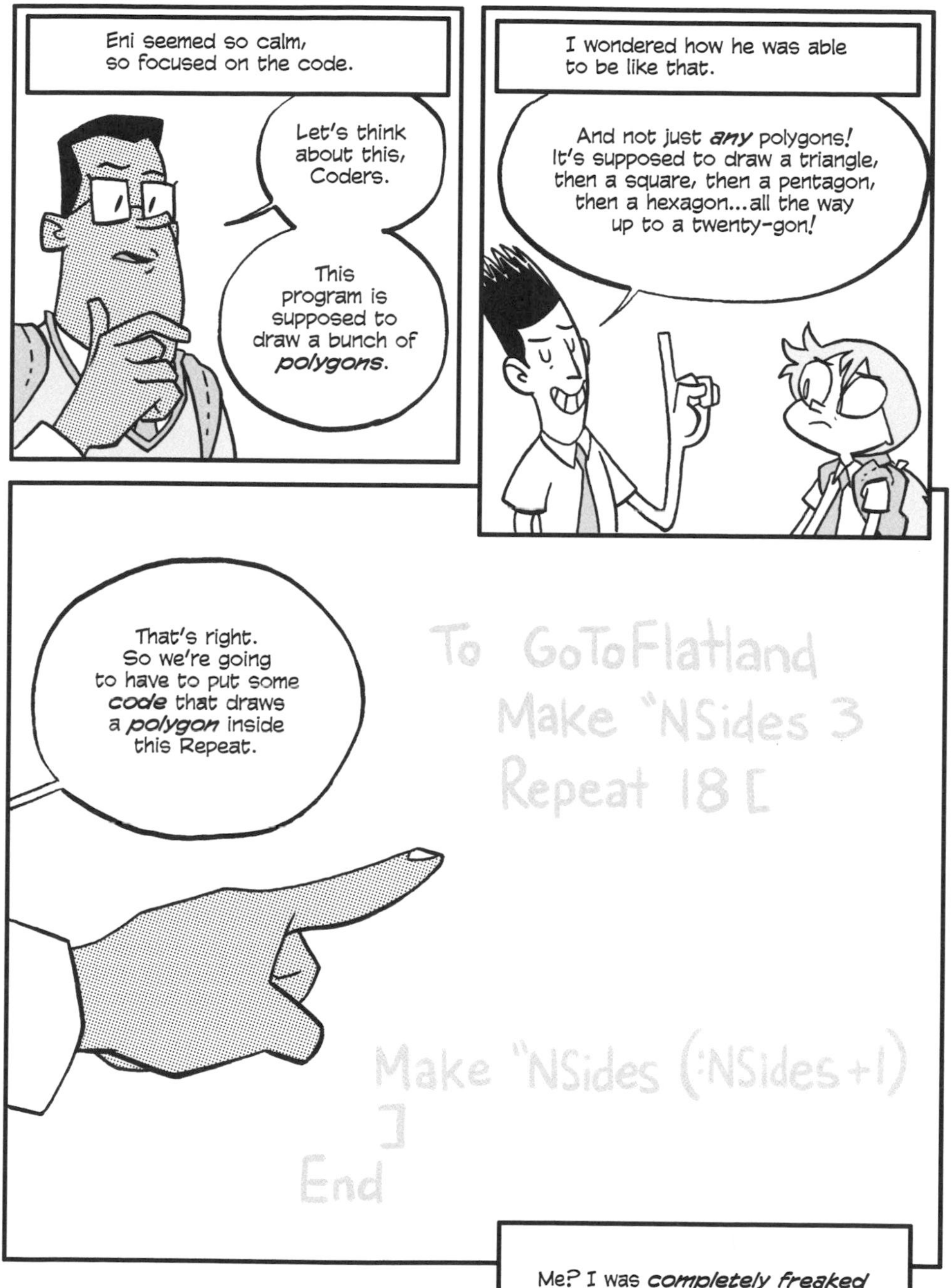
Eni seemed so calm, so focused on the code.
Let's think about this, Coders.
This program is supposed to draw a bunch of polygons.
I wondered how he was able to be like that.
And not just any polygons! It's supposed to draw a triangle, then a square, then a pentagon, then a hexagon...all the way up to a twenty-gon!
That's right. So we're going to have to put some code that draws a polygon inside this Repeat.
To GoToFlatland
Make "NSides 3
Repeat 18 [
Make "NSides (:NSides+1)
]
End
Me? I was completely freaked out by the fact that we were trying to open a portal to another dimension!

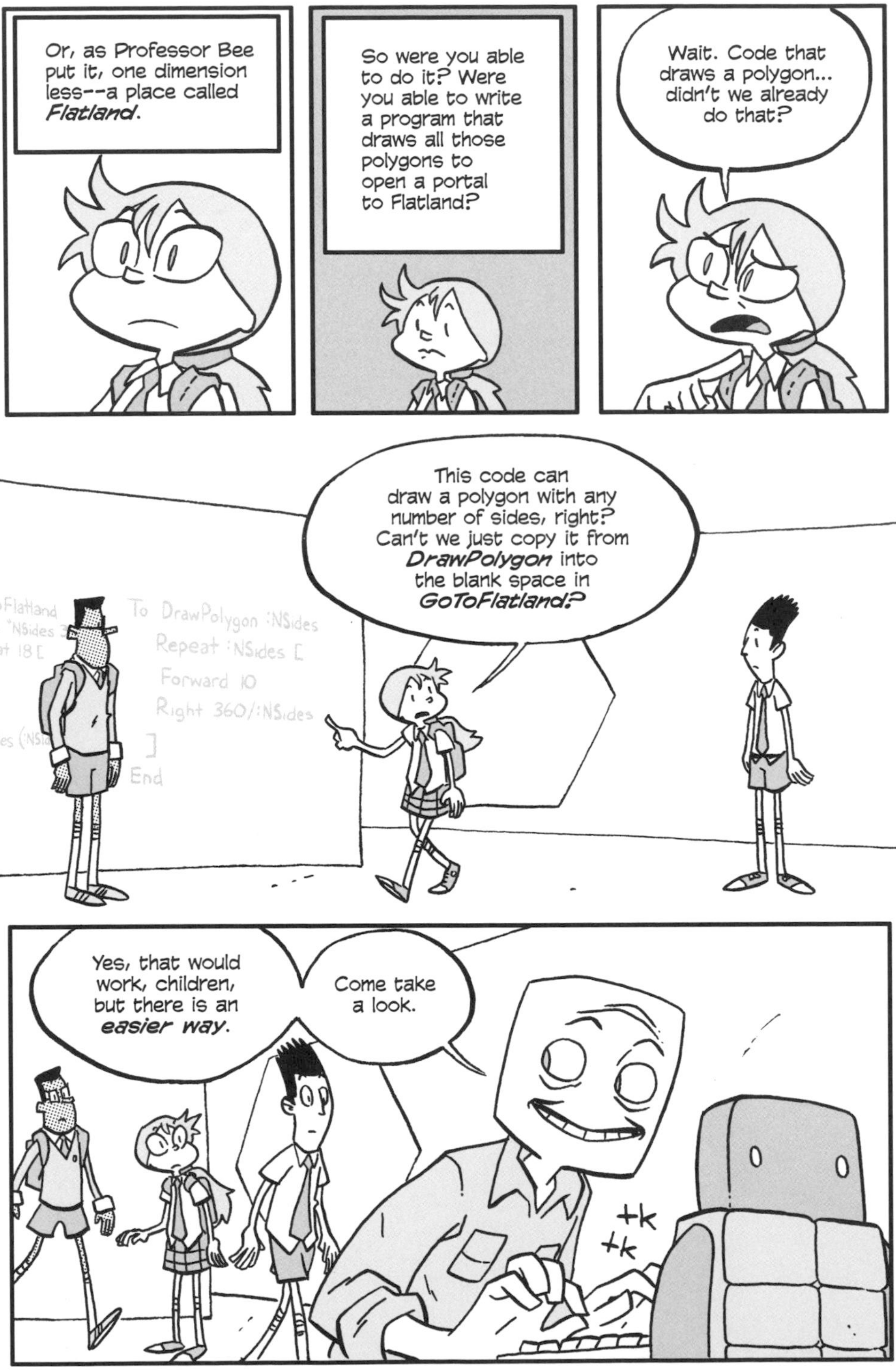

Or, as Professor Bee put it, one dimension less--a place called *Flatland*.
So were you able to do it? Were you able to write a program that draws all those polygons to open a portal to Flatland?
Wait. Code that draws a polygon... didn't we already do that?
This code can draw a polygon with any number of sides, right? Can't we just copy it from *DrawPolygon* into the blank space in *GoToFlatland?*
To GoToFlatland
Repeat 18 [
To DrawPolygon :NSides
Repeat :NSides [
Forward 10
Right 360/:NSides
]
End
Yes, that would work, children, but there is an *easier way*.
Come take a look.
tk
tk

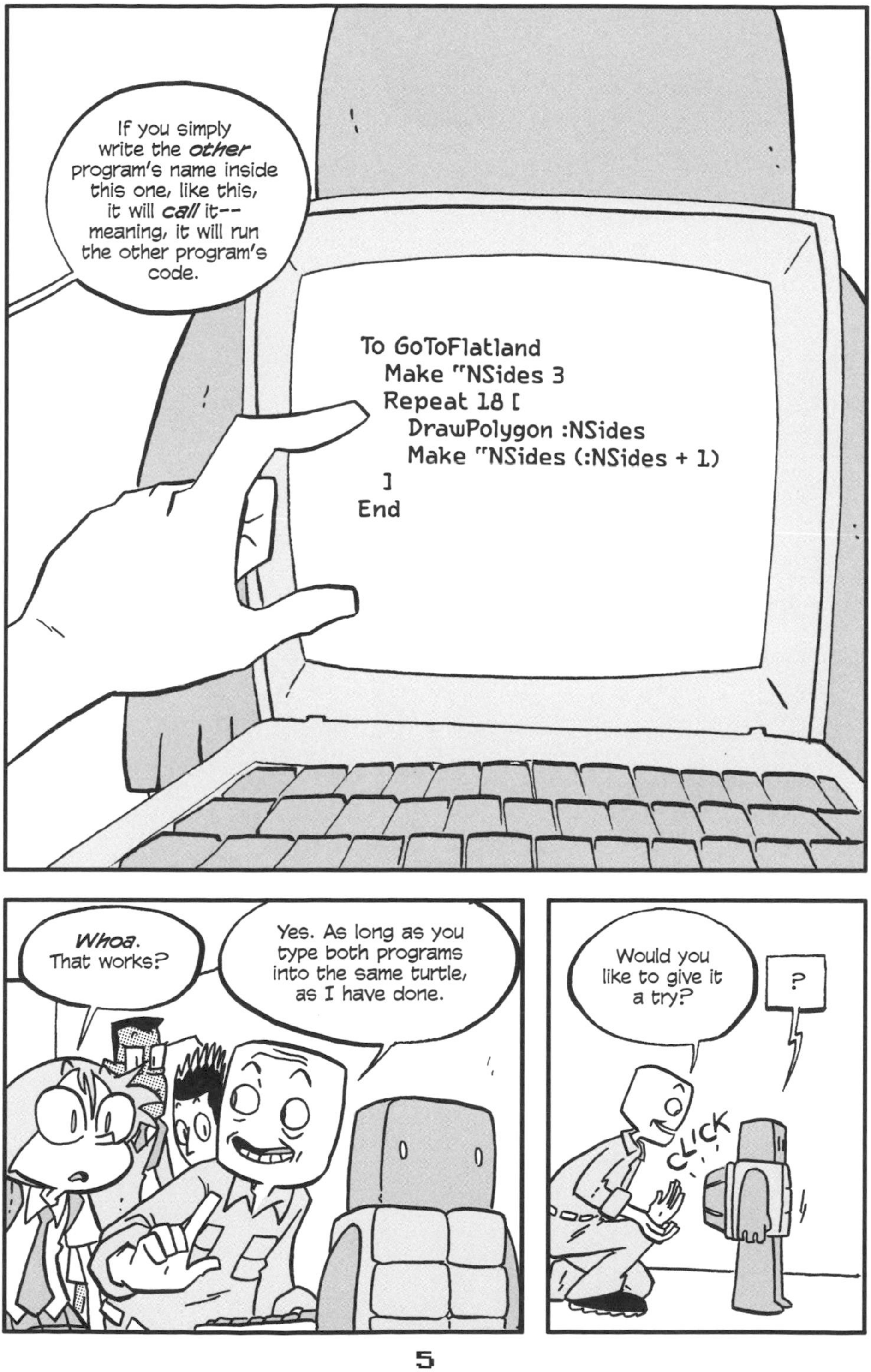

If you simply write the *other* program's name inside this one, like this, it will *call* it-- meaning, it will run the other program's code.
To GoToFlatland
Make "NSides 3
Repeat 18 [
DrawPolygon :NSides
Make "NSides (:NSides + 1)
]
End
Whoa. That works?
Yes. As long as you type both programs into the same turtle, as I have done.
Would you like to give it a try?
?
CLICK

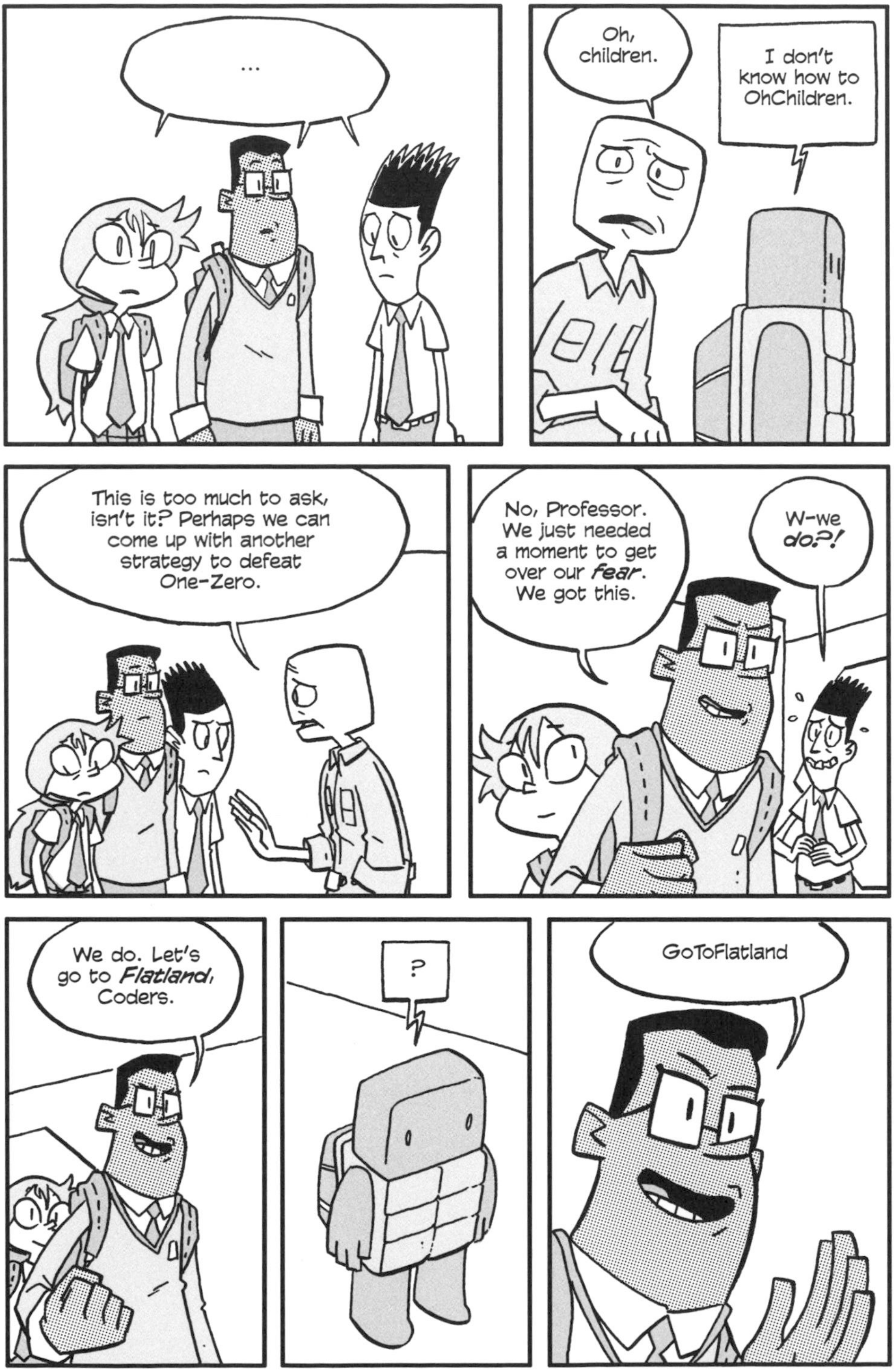
...
Oh, children.
I don't know how to OhChildren.
This is too much to ask, isn't it? Perhaps we can come up with another strategy to defeat One-Zero.
No, Professor. We just needed a moment to get over our *fear*. We got this.
W-we *do?!*
We do. Let's go to *Flatland*, Coders.
?
GoToFlatland

7

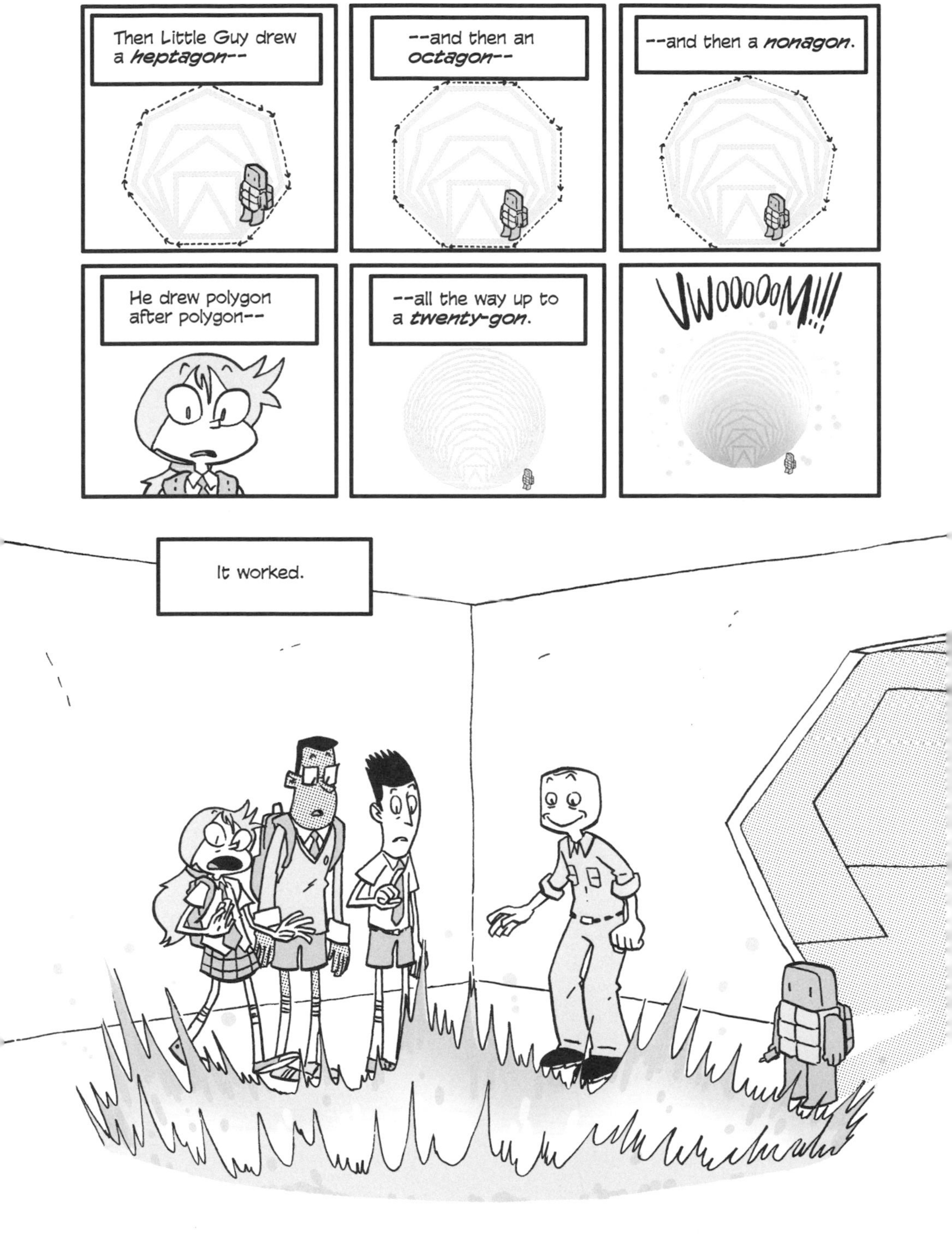
Then Little Guy drew a *heptagon*--
--and then an *octagon*--
--and then a *nonagon*.
He drew polygon after polygon--
--all the way up to a *twenty-gon*.
VWOOOOOOM!!!
It worked.

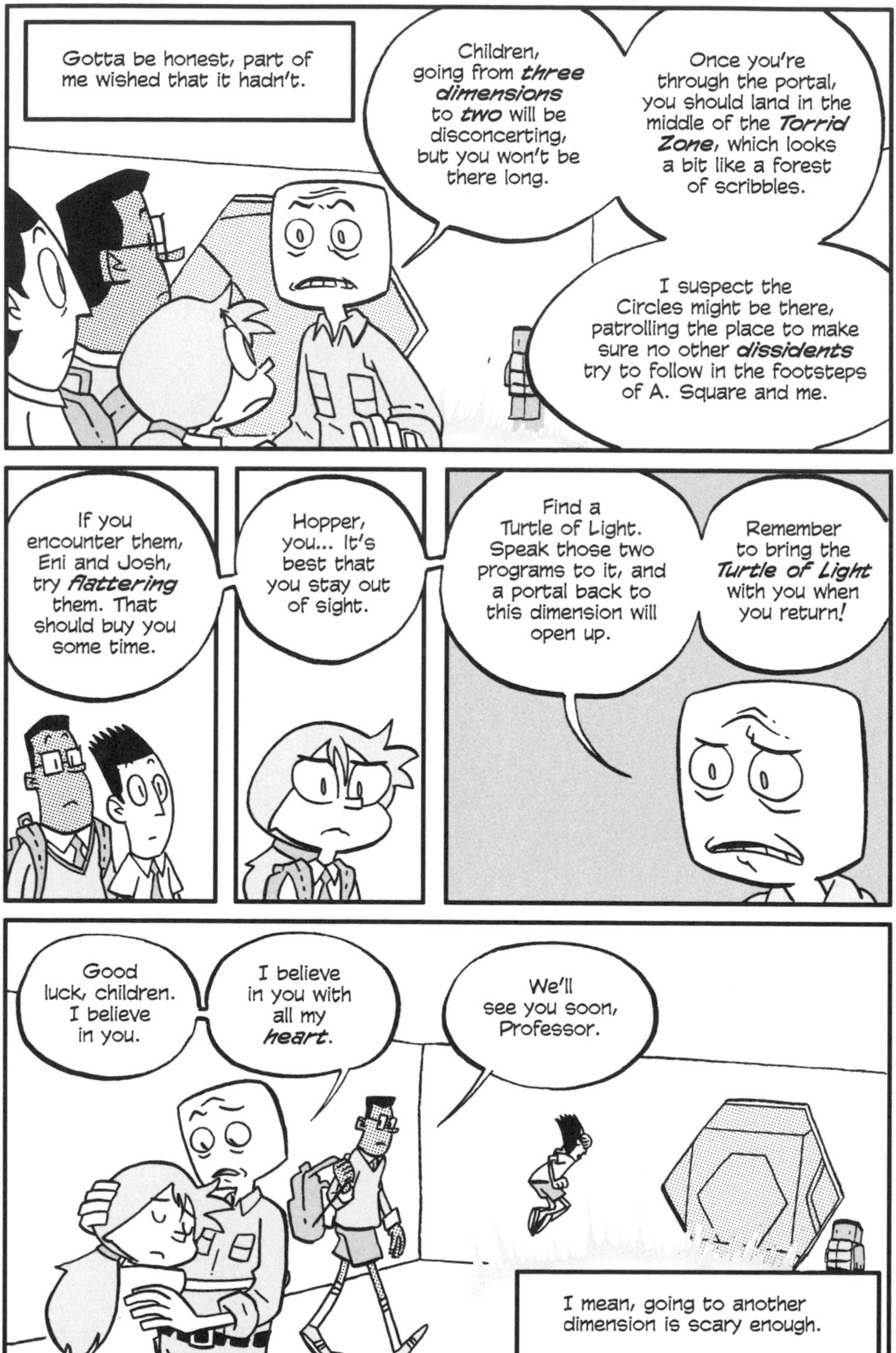

Gotta be honest, part of me wished that it hadn't.
Children, going from *three dimensions* to *two* will be disconcerting, but you won't be there long.
Once you're through the portal, you should land in the middle of the *Torrid Zone*, which looks a bit like a forest of scribbles.
I suspect the Circles might be there, patrolling the place to make sure no other *dissidents* try to follow in the footsteps of A. Square and me.
If you encounter them, Eni and Josh, try *flattering* them. That should buy you some time.
Hopper, you... It's best that you stay out of sight.
Find a Turtle of Light. Speak those two programs to it, and a portal back to this dimension will open up.
Remember to bring the *Turtle of Light* with you when you return!
Good luck, children. I believe in you.
I believe in you with all my *heart*.
We'll see you soon, Professor.
I mean, going to another dimension is scary enough.

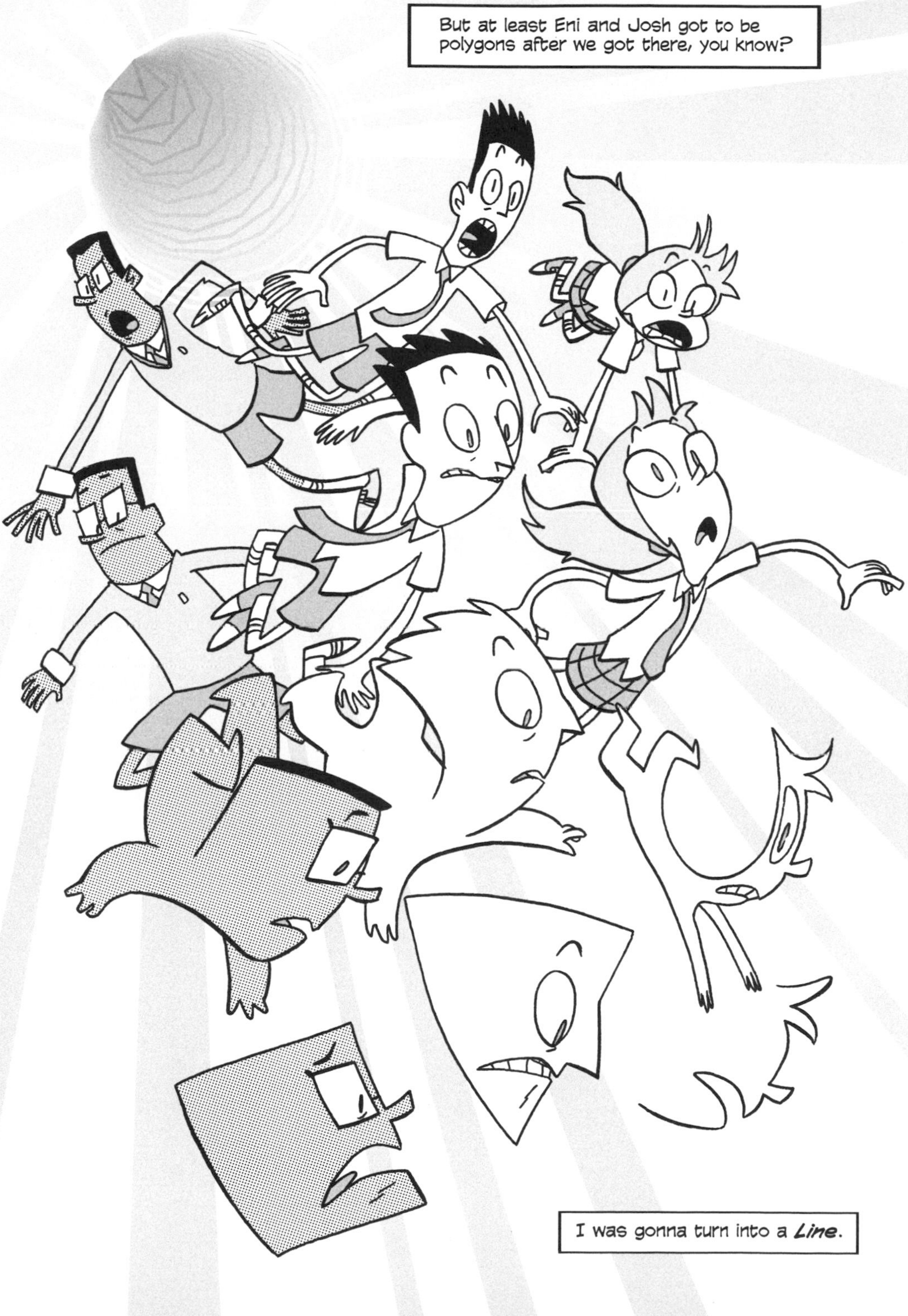
But at least Eni and Josh got to be polygons after we got there, you know?
I was gonna turn into a *Line*.

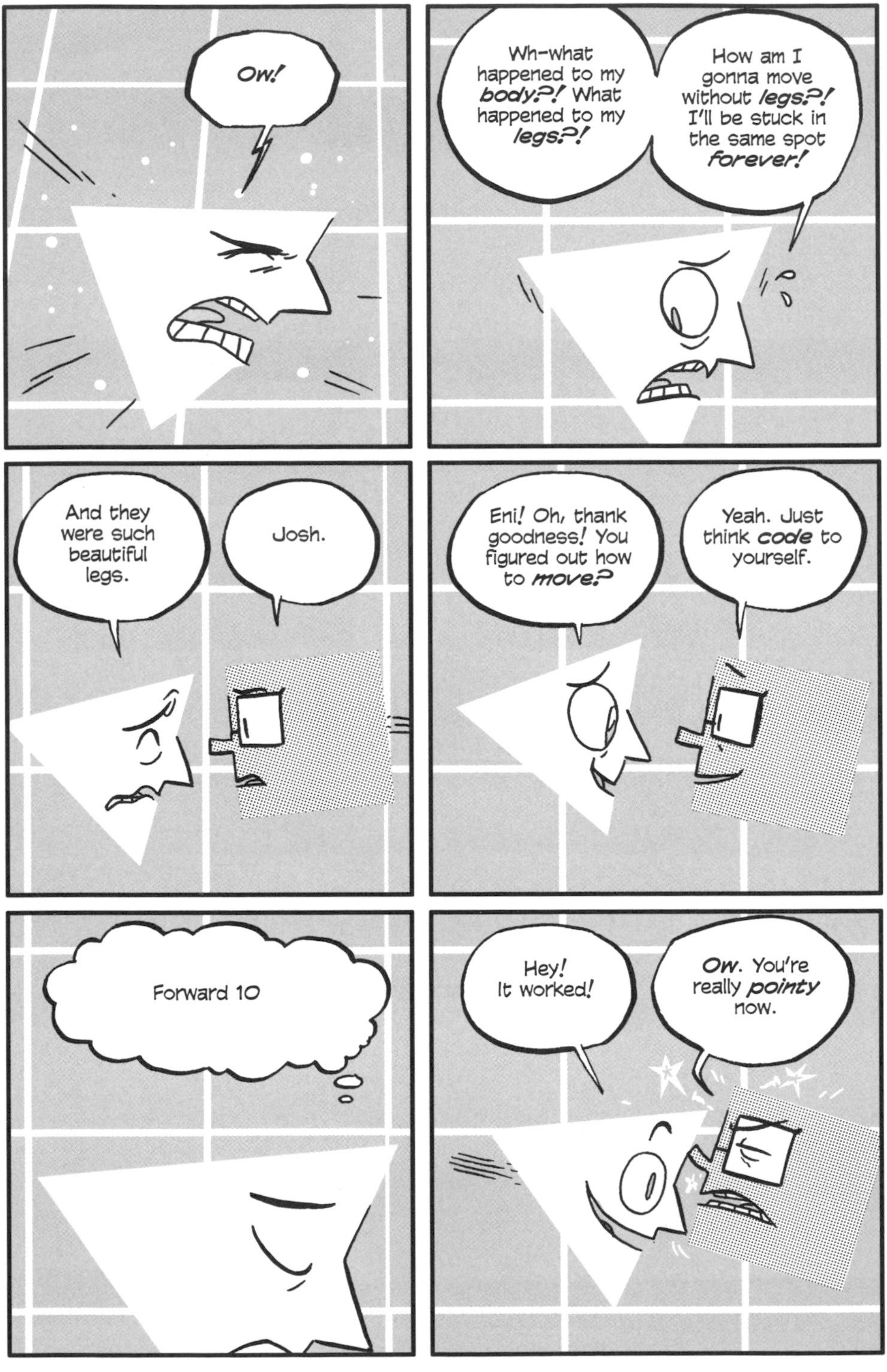
Ow!
Wh-what happened to my body?! What happened to my legs?!
How am I gonna move without legs?! I'll be stuck in the same spot forever!
And they were such beautiful legs.
Josh.
Eni! Oh, thank goodness! You figured out how to move?
Yeah. Just think code to yourself.
Forward 10
Hey! It worked!
Ow. You're really pointy now.

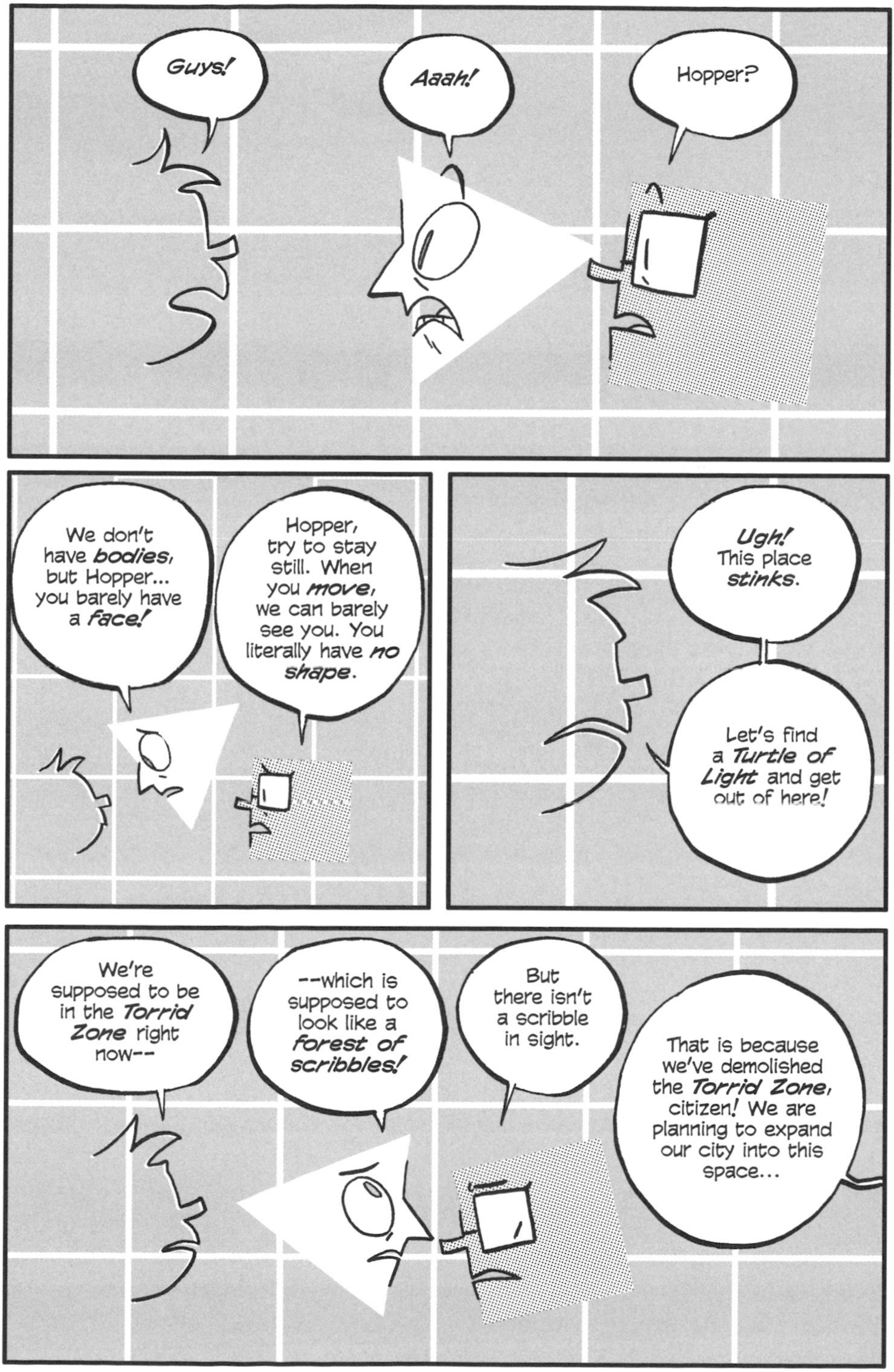
Guys!
Aaah!
Hopper?
We don't have bodies, but Hopper... you barely have a face!
Hopper, try to stay still. When you move, we can barely see you. You literally have no shape.
Ugh! This place stinks.
Let's find a Turtle of Light and get out of here!
We're supposed to be in the Torrid Zone right now--
--which is supposed to look like a forest of scribbles!
But there isn't a scribble in sight.
That is because we've demolished the Torrid Zone, citizen! We are planning to expand our city into this space...

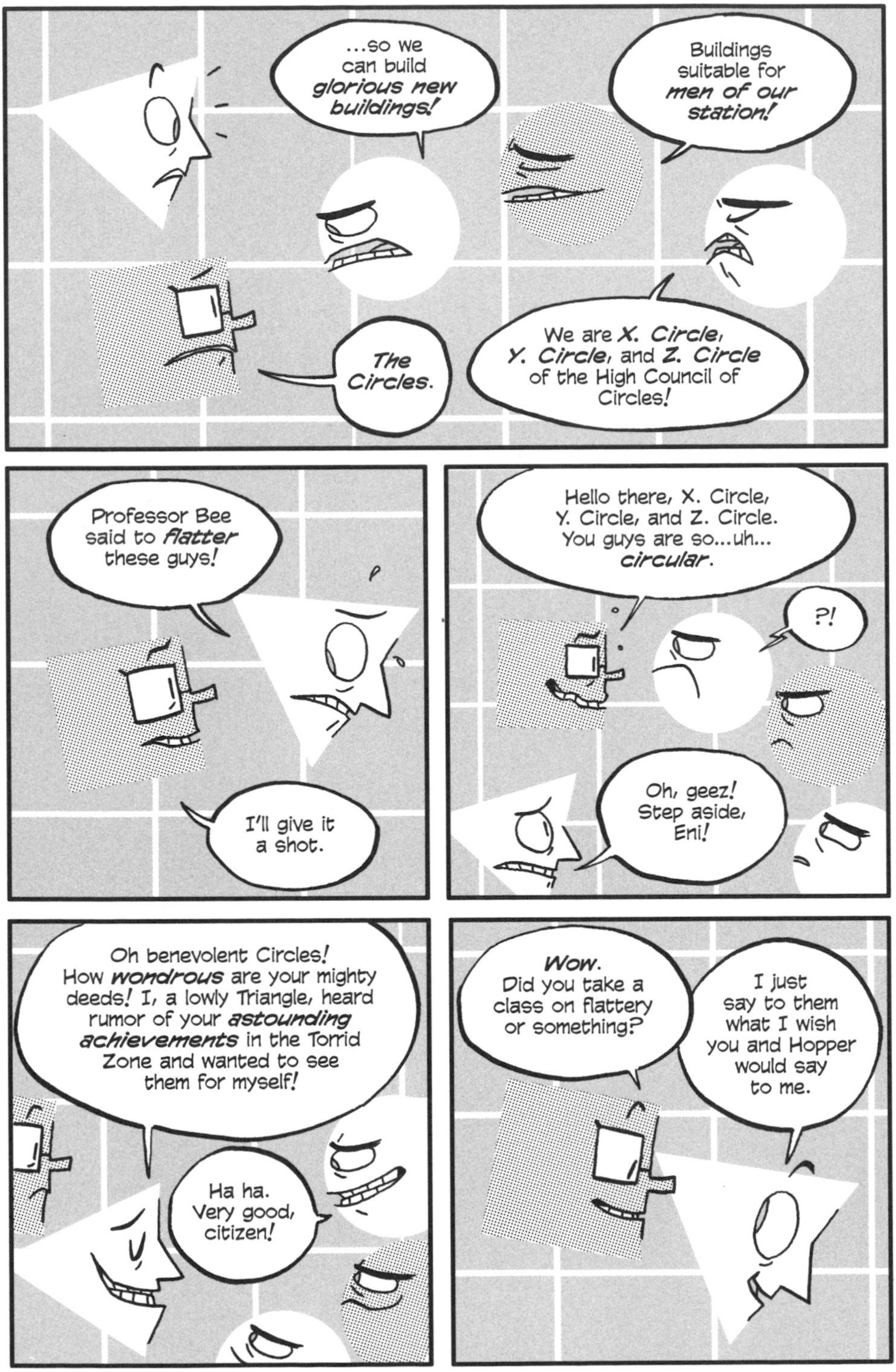
...so we can build *glorious new buildings!*
Buildings suitable for *men of our station!*
The Circles.
We are *X. Circle*, *Y. Circle*, and *Z. Circle* of the High Council of Circles!
Professor Bee said to *flatter* these guys!
I'll give it a shot.
Hello there, X. Circle, Y. Circle, and Z. Circle. You guys are so...uh... *circular*.
?!
Oh, geez! Step aside, Eni!
Oh benevolent Circles! How *wondrous* are your mighty deeds! I, a lowly Triangle, heard rumor of your *astounding achievements* in the Torrid Zone and wanted to see them for myself!
Ha ha. Very good, citizen!
Wow. Did you take a class on flattery or something?
I just say to them what I wish you and Hopper would say to me.

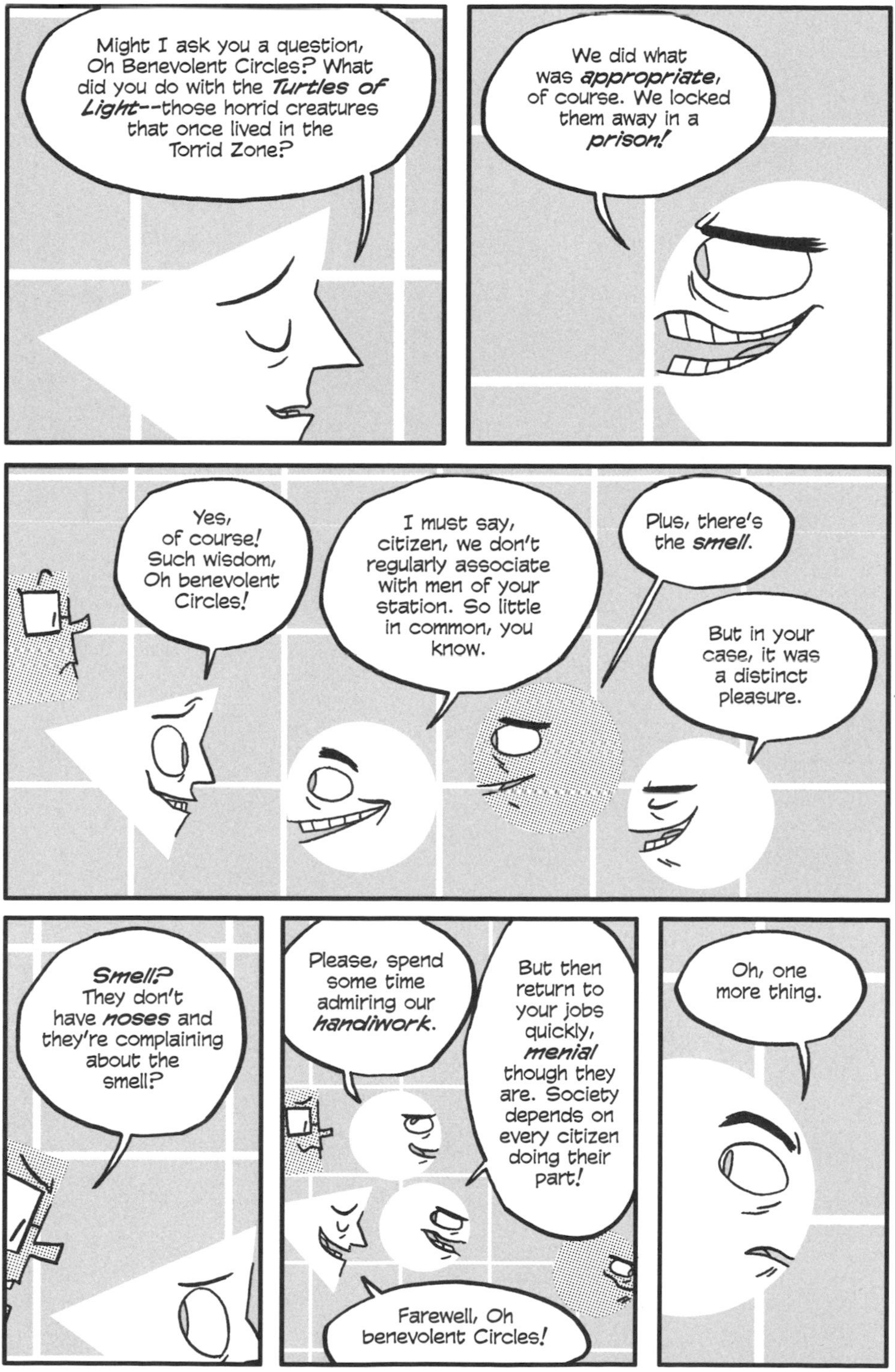

Might I ask you a question, Oh Benevolent Circles? What did you do with the *Turtles of Light*--those horrid creatures that once lived in the Torrid Zone?
We did what was *appropriate*, of course. We locked them away in a *prison!*
Yes, of course! Such wisdom, Oh benevolent Circles!
I must say, citizen, we don't regularly associate with men of your station. So little in common, you know.
Plus, there's the *smell*.
But in your case, it was a distinct pleasure.
Smell? They don't have *noses* and they're complaining about the smell?
Please, spend some time admiring our *handiwork*.
But then return to your jobs quickly, *menial* though they are. Society depends on every citizen doing their part!
Farewell, Oh benevolent Circles!
Oh, one more thing.

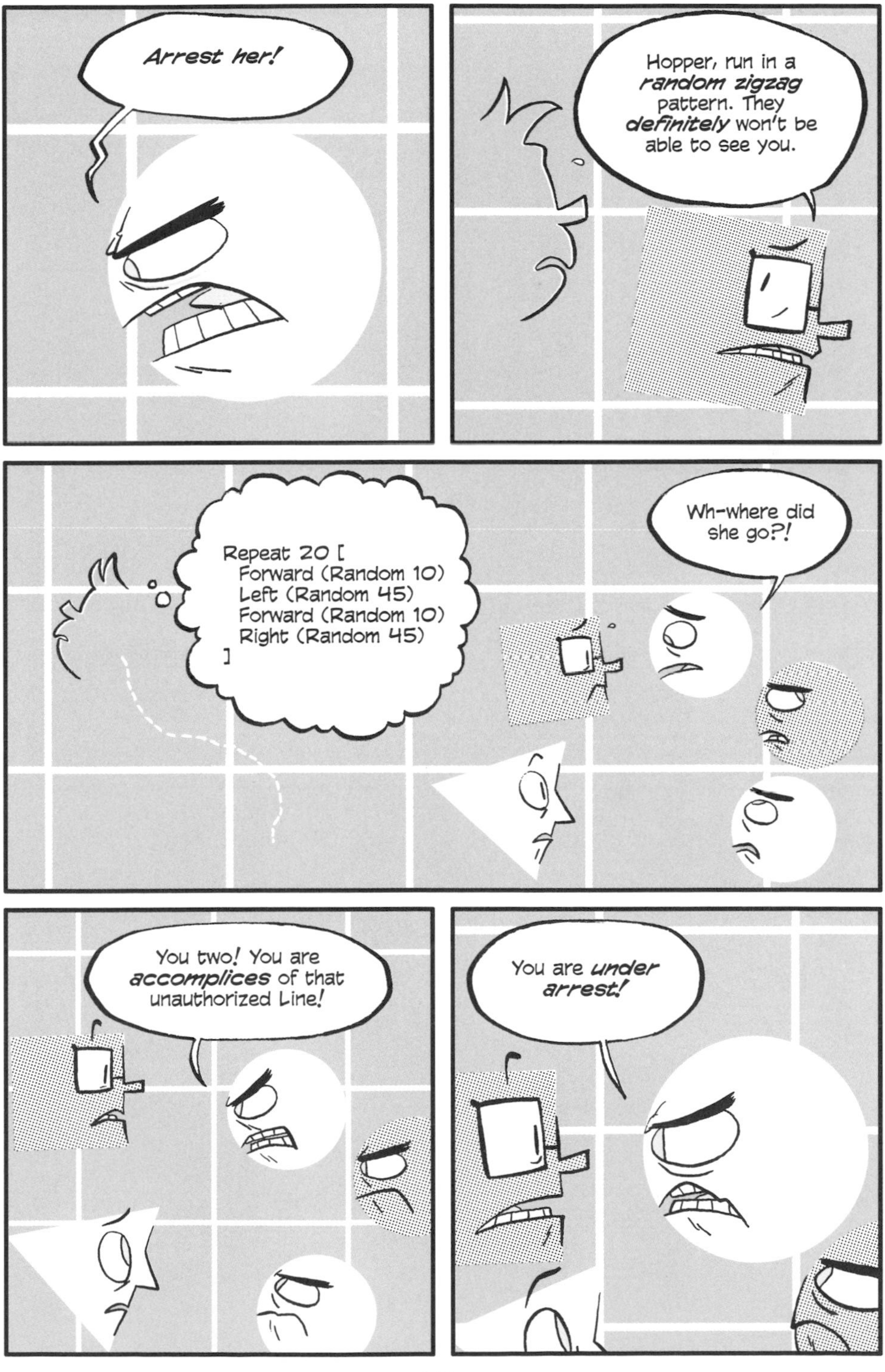
Arrest her!
Hopper, run in a *random zigzag* pattern. They *definitely* won't be able to see you.
Repeat 20 [
Forward (Random 10)
Left (Random 45)
Forward (Random 10)
Right (Random 45)
]
Wh-where did she go?!
You two! You are *accomplices* of that unauthorized Line!
You are *under arrest!*

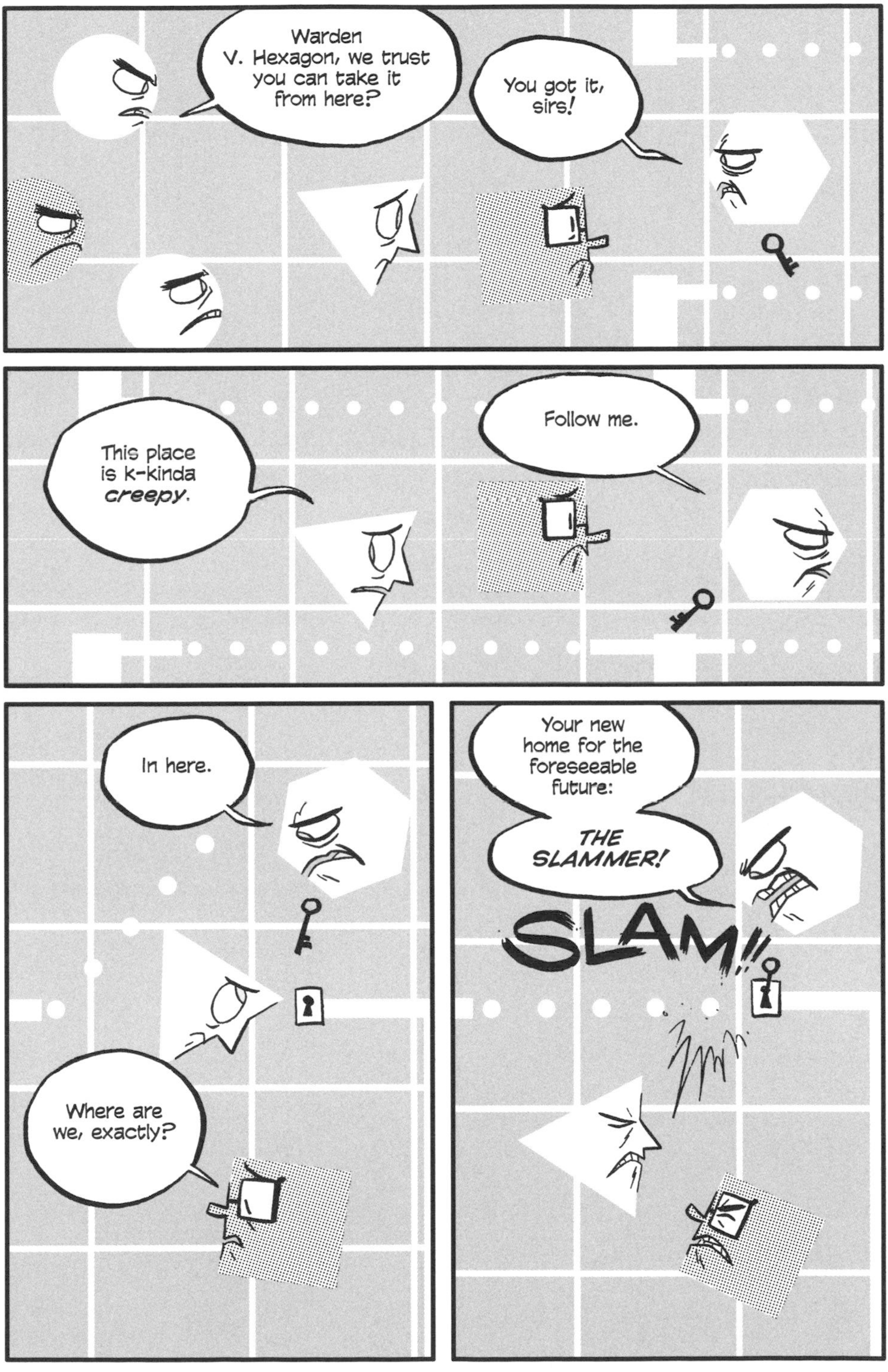
Warden V. Hexagon, we trust you can take it from here?
You got it, sirs!
This place is k-kinda *creepy*.
Follow me.
In here.
Where are we, exactly?
Your new home for the foreseeable future:
THE SLAMMER!
SLAM!!

Ha ha! *Yes!*
Hey! What's all that commotion?!
Oh no! *The warden!*
Hold on one hot second! What's that Square doing in *this* cell?! I coulda *sworn* I put the Square criminal in the other cell, with the Triangle criminal!
?

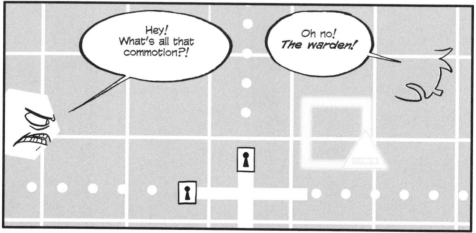

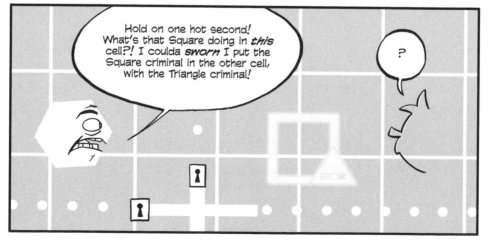

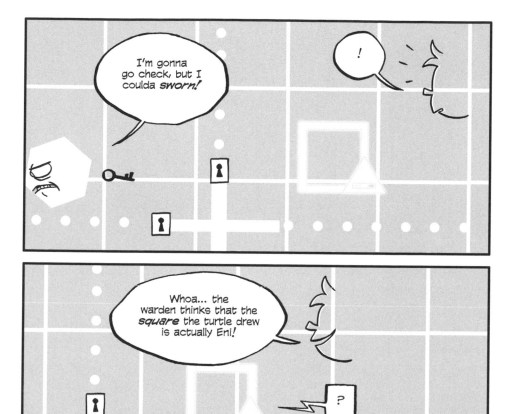

I'm gonna go check, but I coulda *sworn!*

!

Whoa... the warden thinks that the *square* the turtle drew is actually Eni!

?

Right then and there, a plan formed in my head.

I just need to come up with code that draws three circles side by side, each with a radius of 10 steps!

ClearScreen

CLEAR!

We're at another one of those points in the story again. Do you think you can write the code I described?

Can you get the Turtle of Light to draw three circles side by side?

Chapter

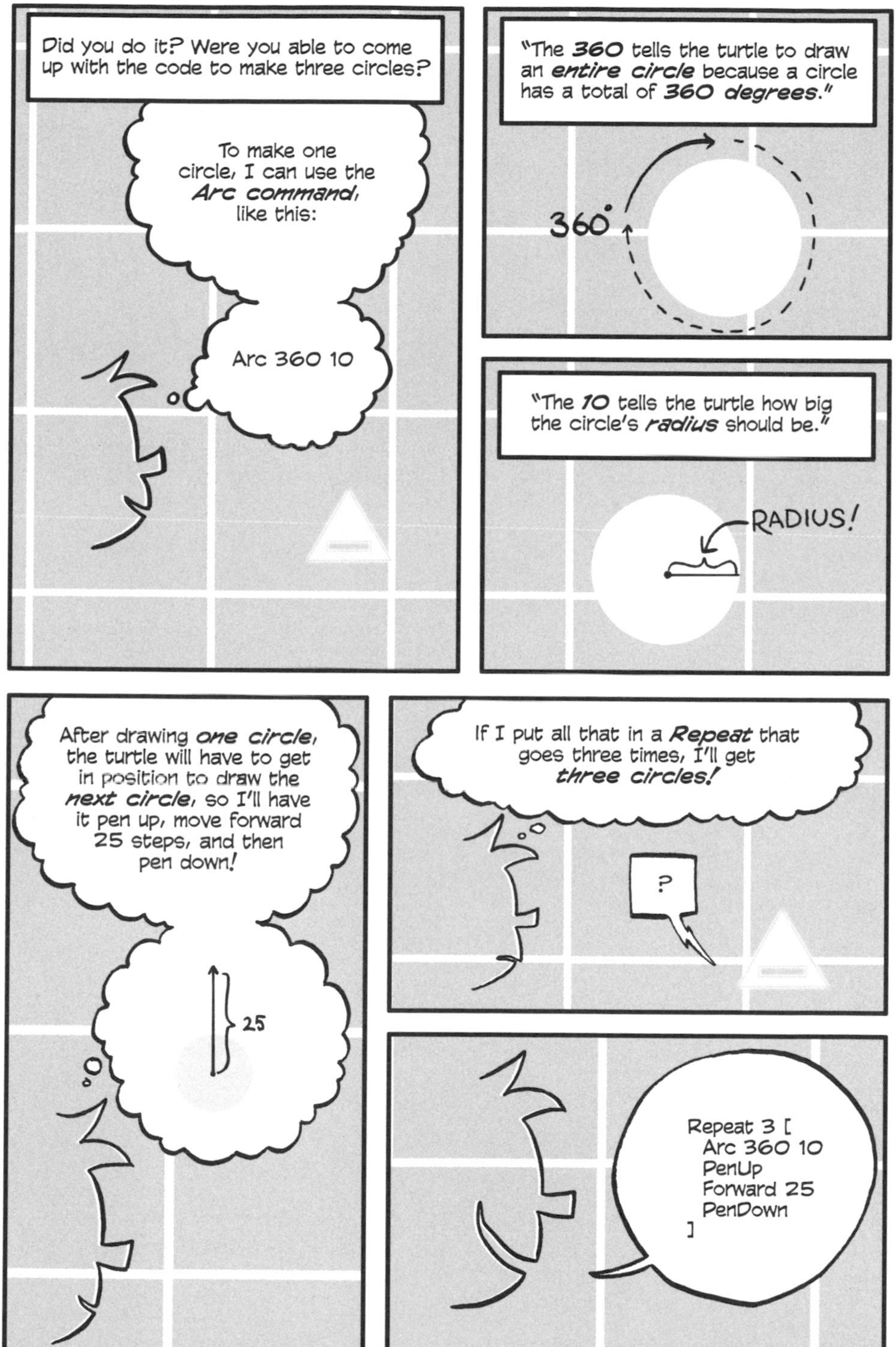
Did you do it? Were you able to come up with the code to make three circles?
To make one circle, I can use the *Arc command*, like this:
Arc 360 10
"The **360** tells the turtle to draw an ***entire circle*** because a circle has a total of ***360 degrees***."
360°
"The *10* tells the turtle how big the circle's ***radius*** should be."
RADIUS!
After drawing ***one circle***, the turtle will have to get in position to draw the ***next circle***, so I'll have it pen up, move forward 25 steps, and then pen down!
25
If I put all that in a ***Repeat*** that goes three times, I'll get ***three circles!***
?
Repeat 3 [
Arc 360 10
PenUp
Forward 25
PenDown
]

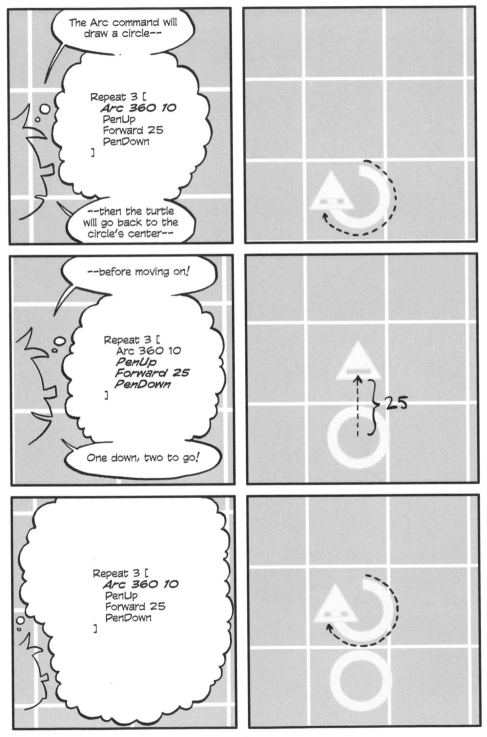

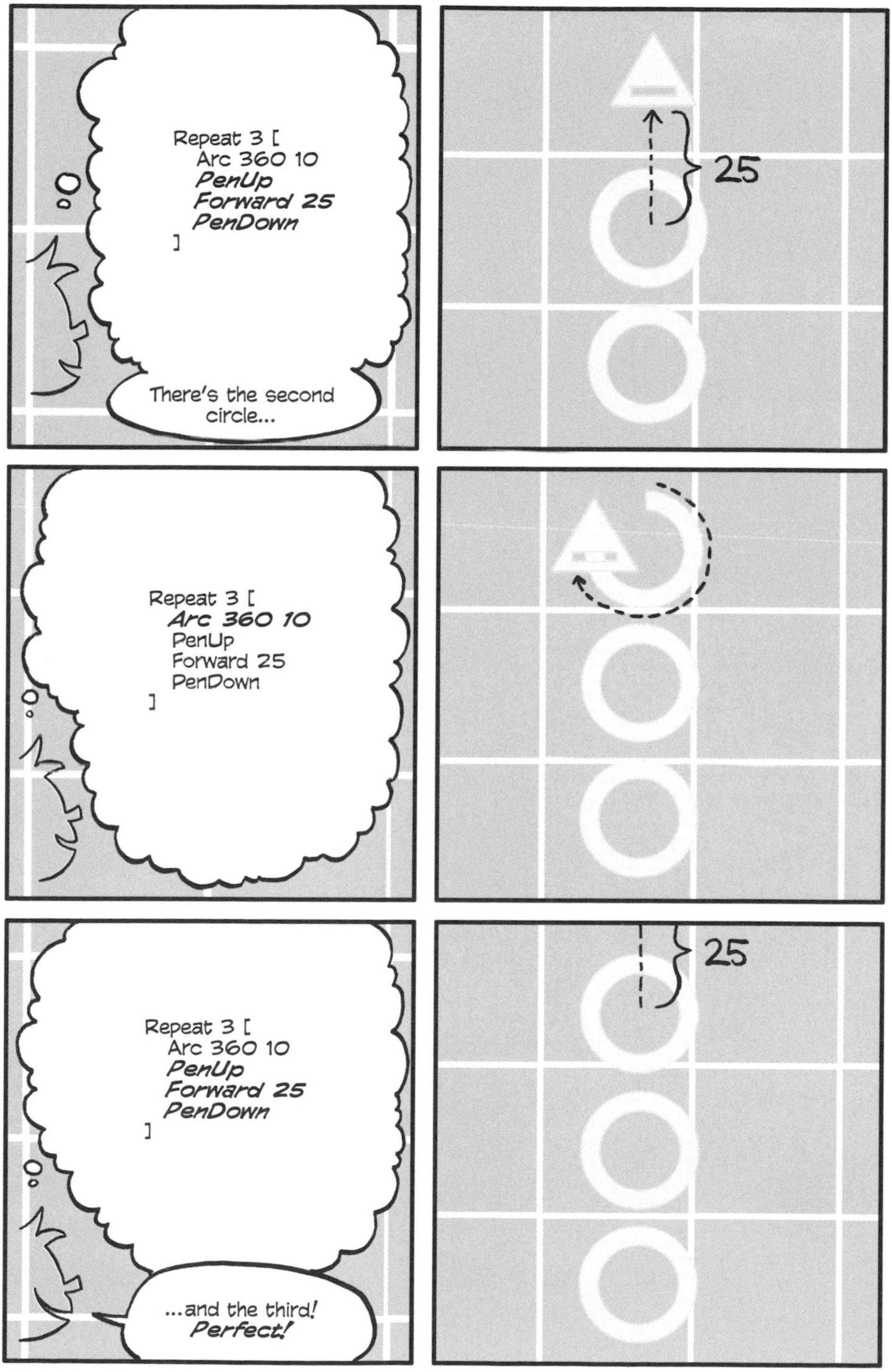

Repeat 3 [
Arc 360 10
PenUp
Forward 25
PenDown
]
There's the second circle...
25
Repeat 3 [
Arc 360 10
PenUp
Forward 25
PenDown
]
25
Repeat 3 [
Arc 360 10
PenUp
Forward 25
PenDown
]
...and the third! *Perfect!*

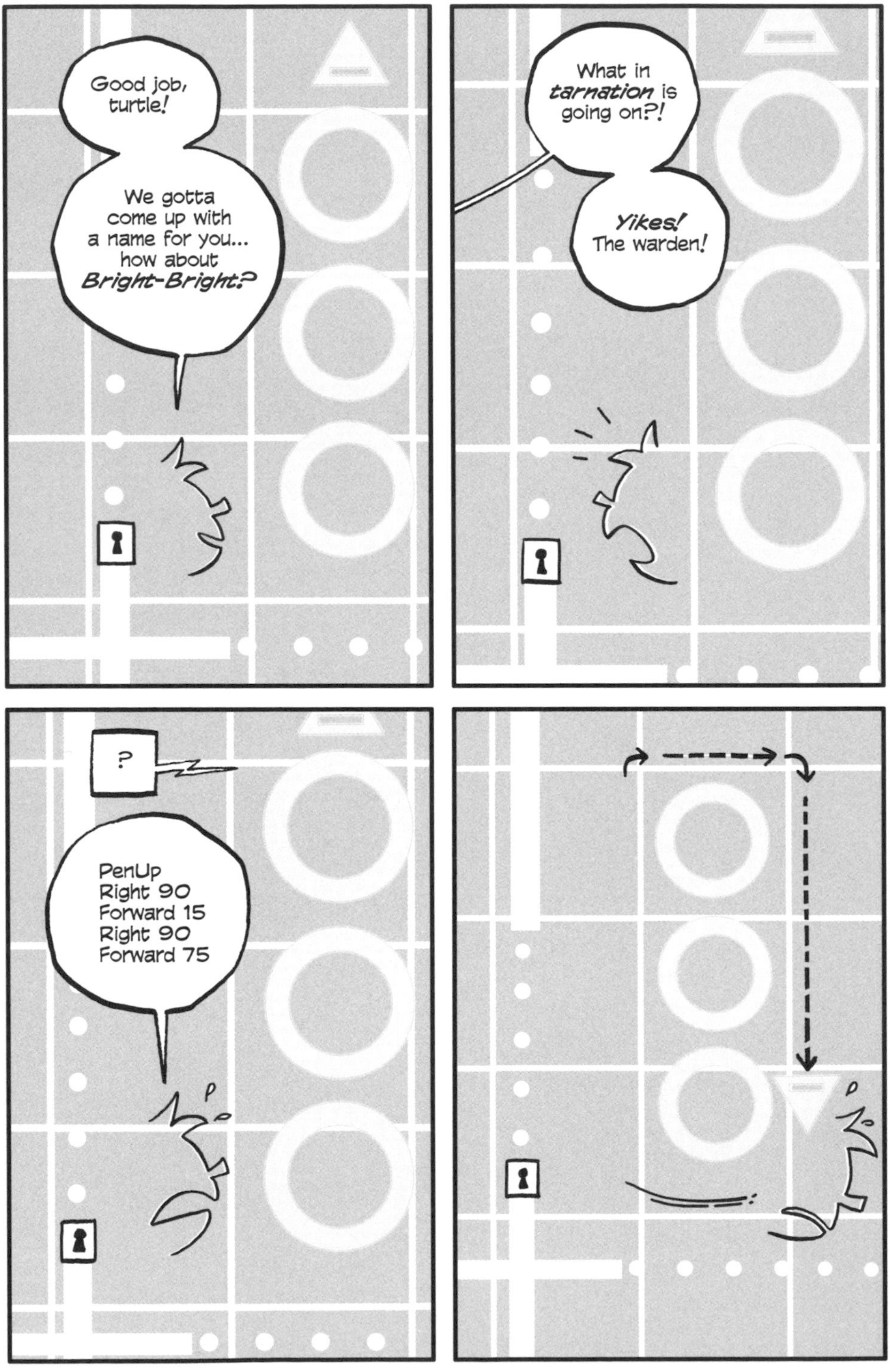
Good job, turtle!
We gotta come up with a name for you... how about *Bright-Bright?*
What in *tarnation* is going on?!
Yikes! The warden!
?
PenUp
Right 90
Forward 15
Right 90
Forward 75

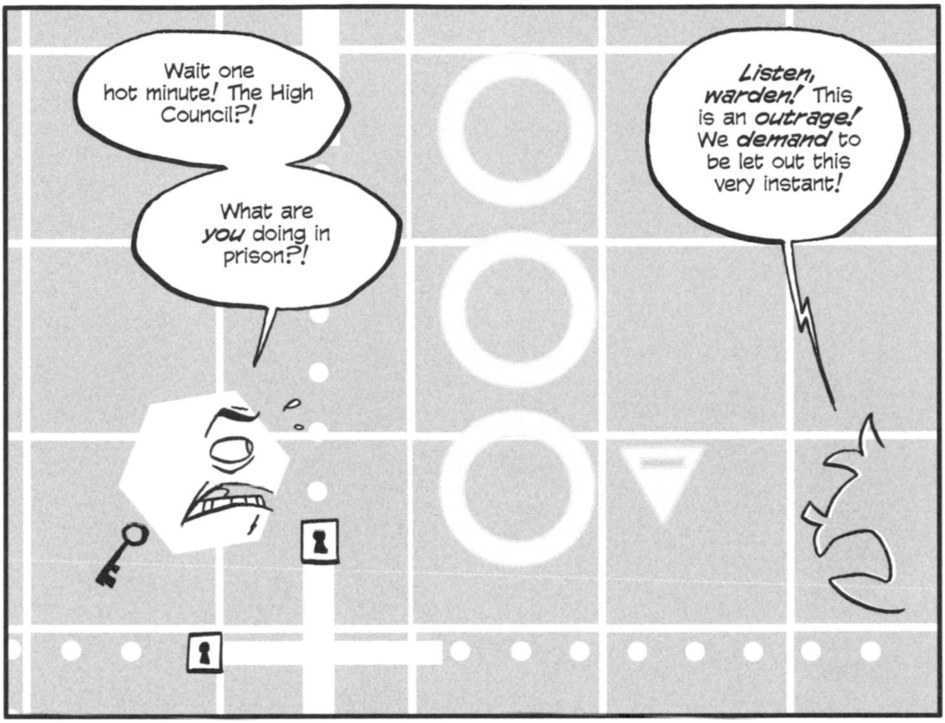
Wait one hot minute! The High Council?!
What are *you* doing in prison?!
Listen, warden! This is an ***outrage!*** We ***demand*** to be let out this very instant!

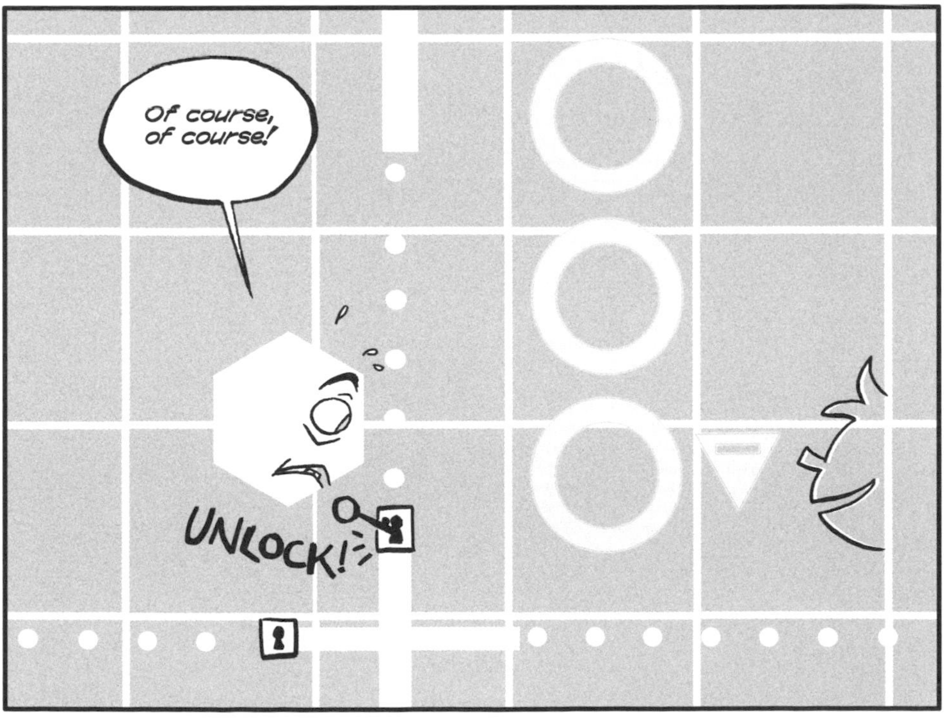
Of course, of course!
UNLOCK!

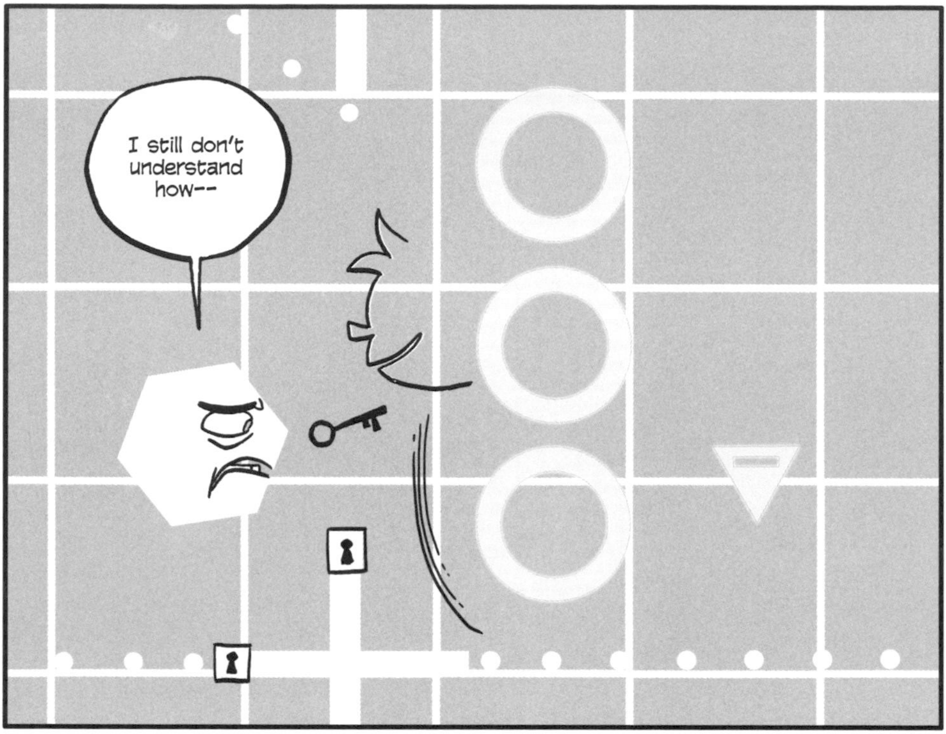
I still don't understand how--

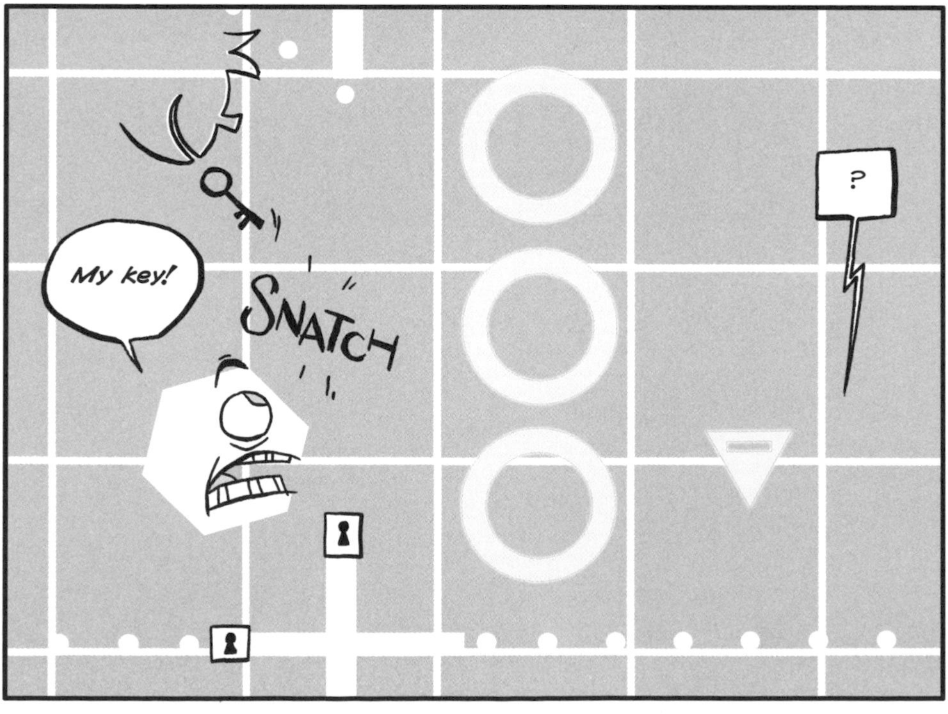
My key!
SNATCH
?

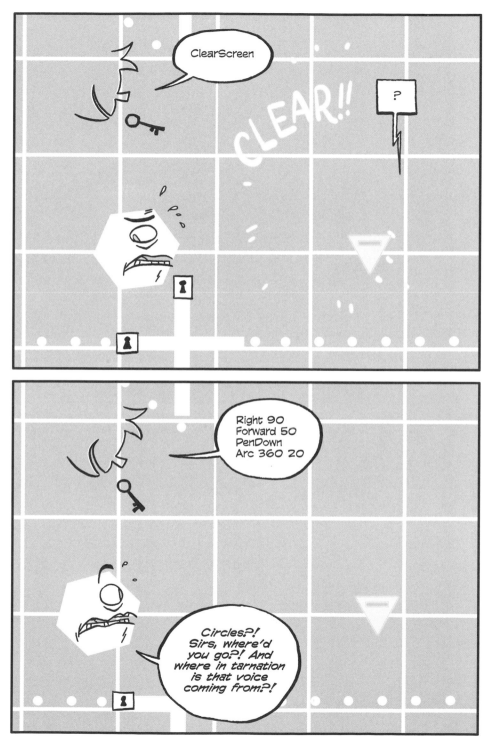

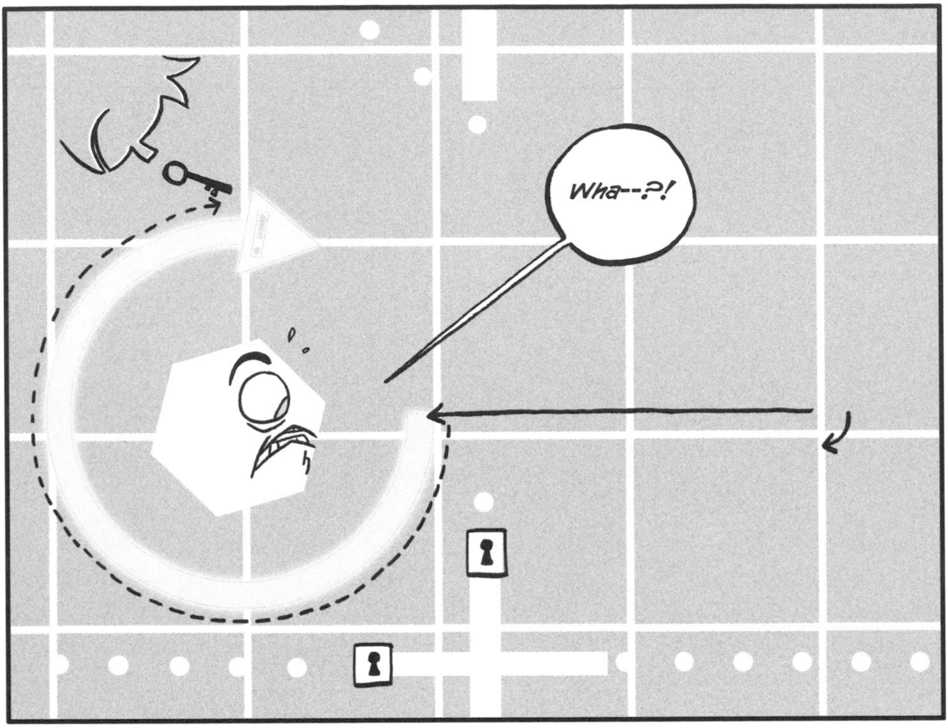
Wha--?!

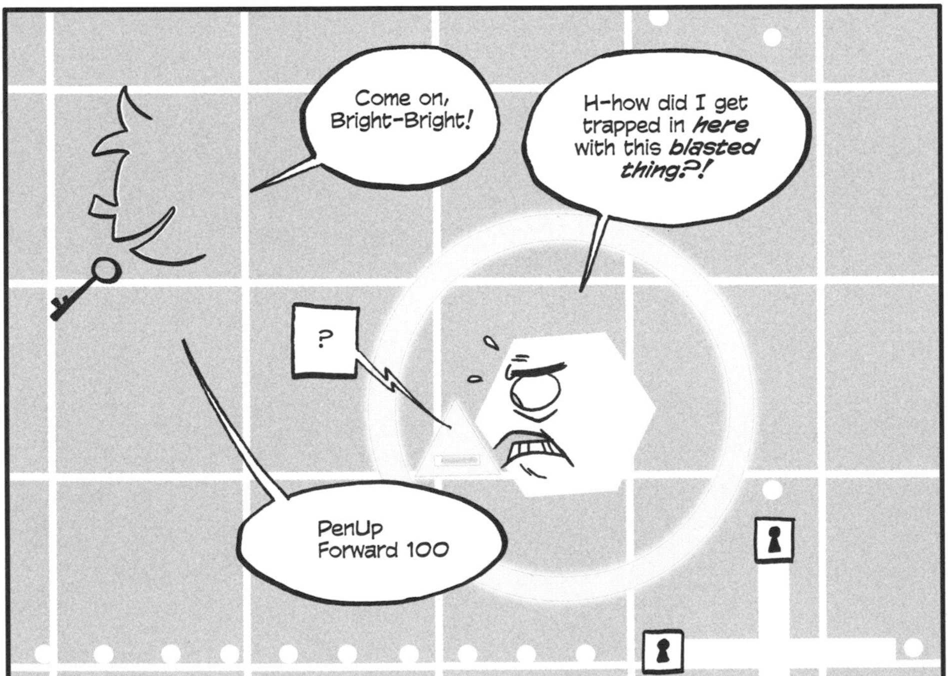
Come on, Bright-Bright!
H-how did I get trapped in *here* with this *blasted* thing?!
?
PenUp Forward 100

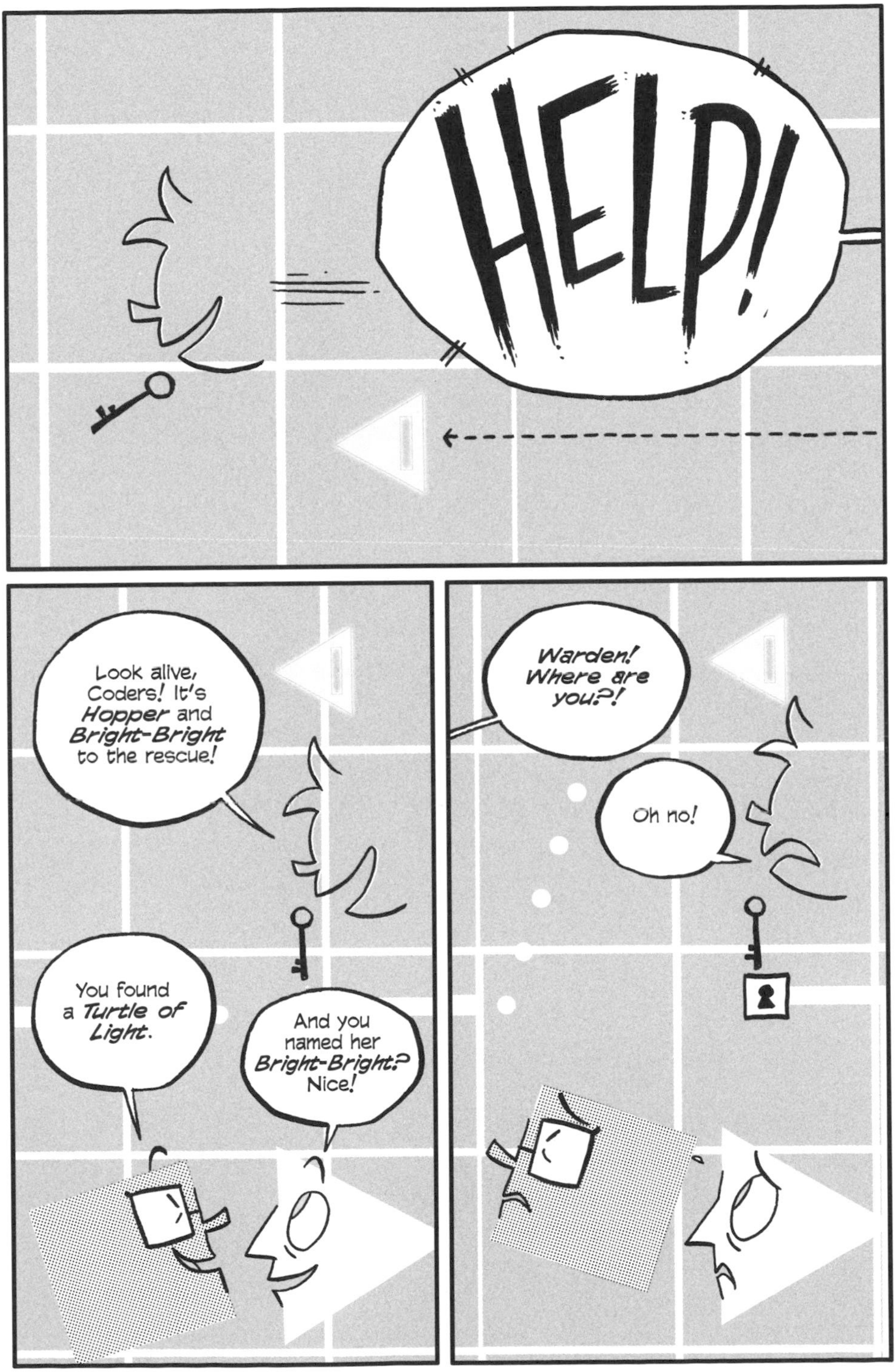
HELP!
Look alive, Coders! It's *Hopper* and *Bright-Bright* to the rescue!
You found a *Turtle of Light*.
And you named her *Bright-Bright?* Nice!
Warden! Where are you?!
Oh no!

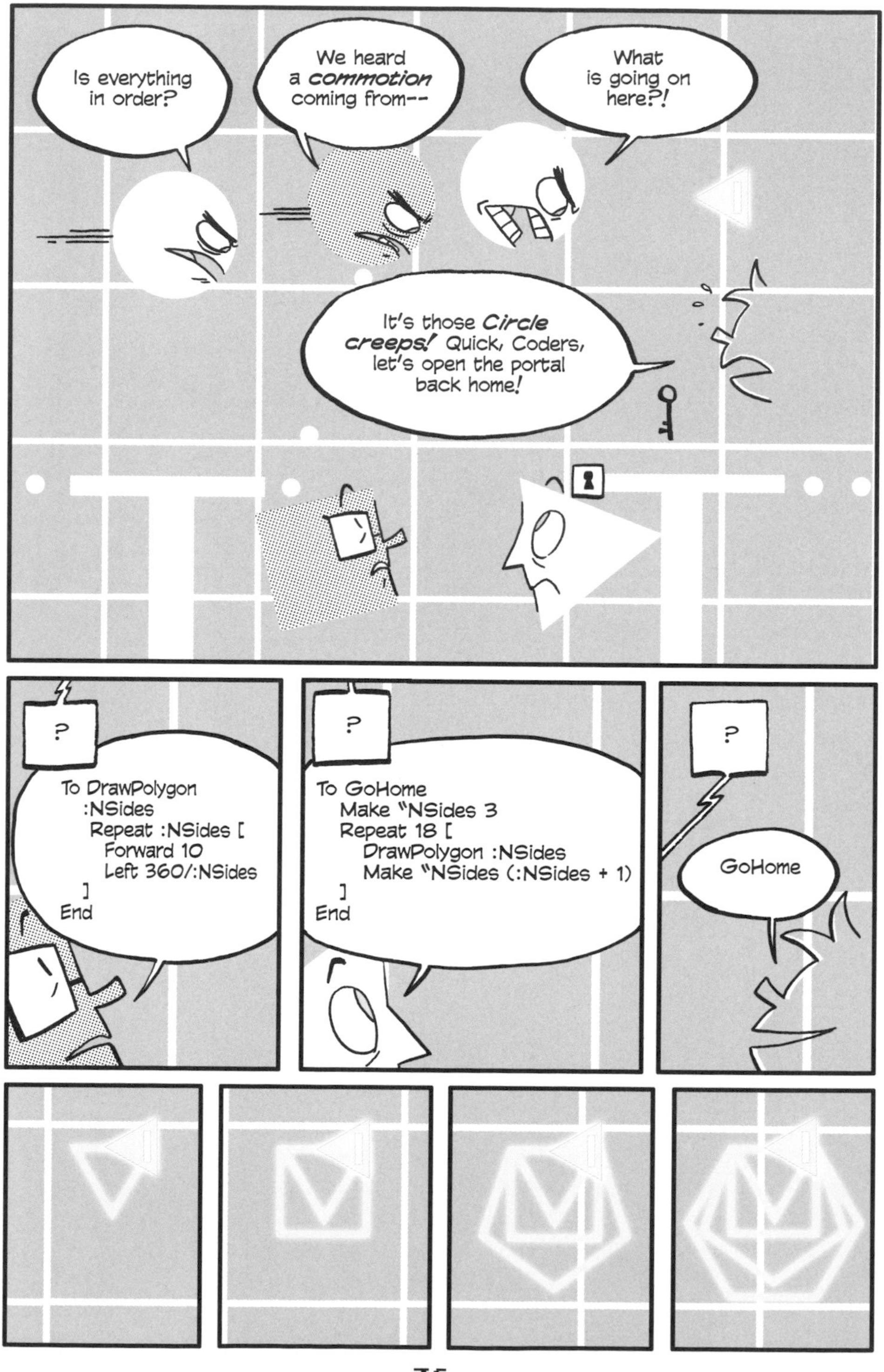
Is everything in order?
We heard a **commotion** coming from--
What is going on here?!
It's those ***Circle creeps!*** Quick, Coders, let's open the portal back home!
?
To DrawPolygon :NSides
Repeat :NSides [
Forward 10
Left 360/:NSides
]
End
?
To GoHome
Make "NSides 3
Repeat 18 [
DrawPolygon :NSides
Make "NSides (:NSides + 1)
]
End
?
GoHome

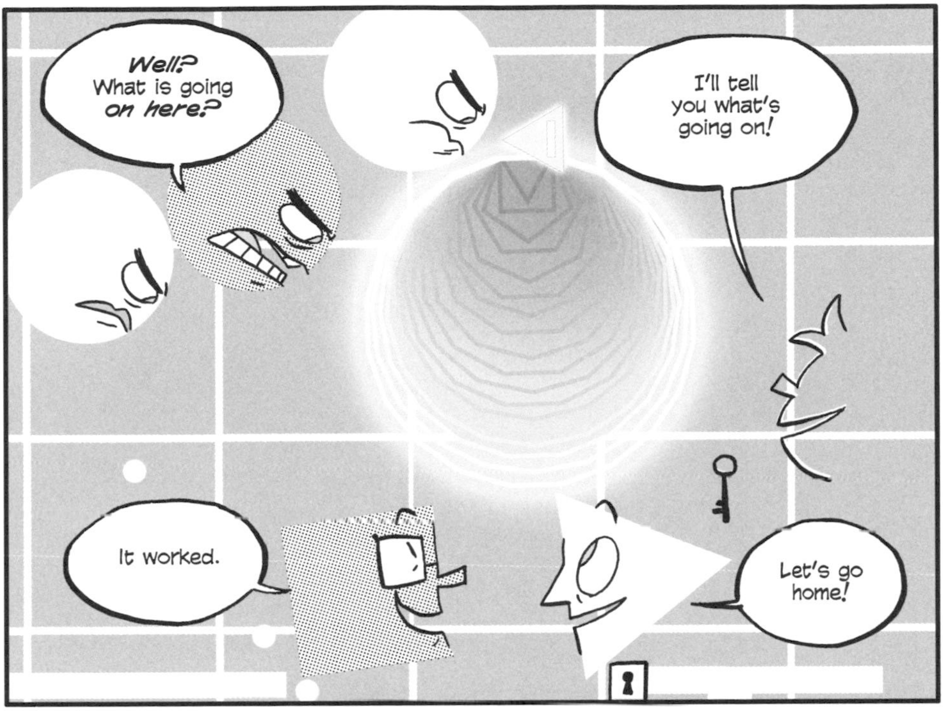
Well? What is going on here?
I'll tell you what's going on!
It worked.
Let's go home!

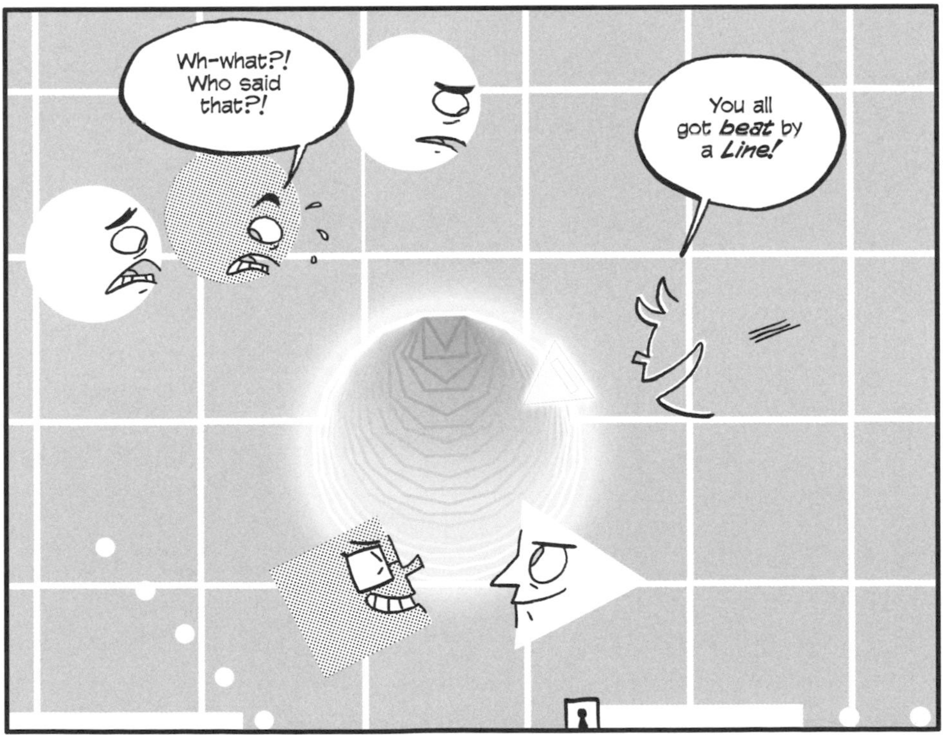
Wh-what?! Who said that?!
You all got beat by a Line!

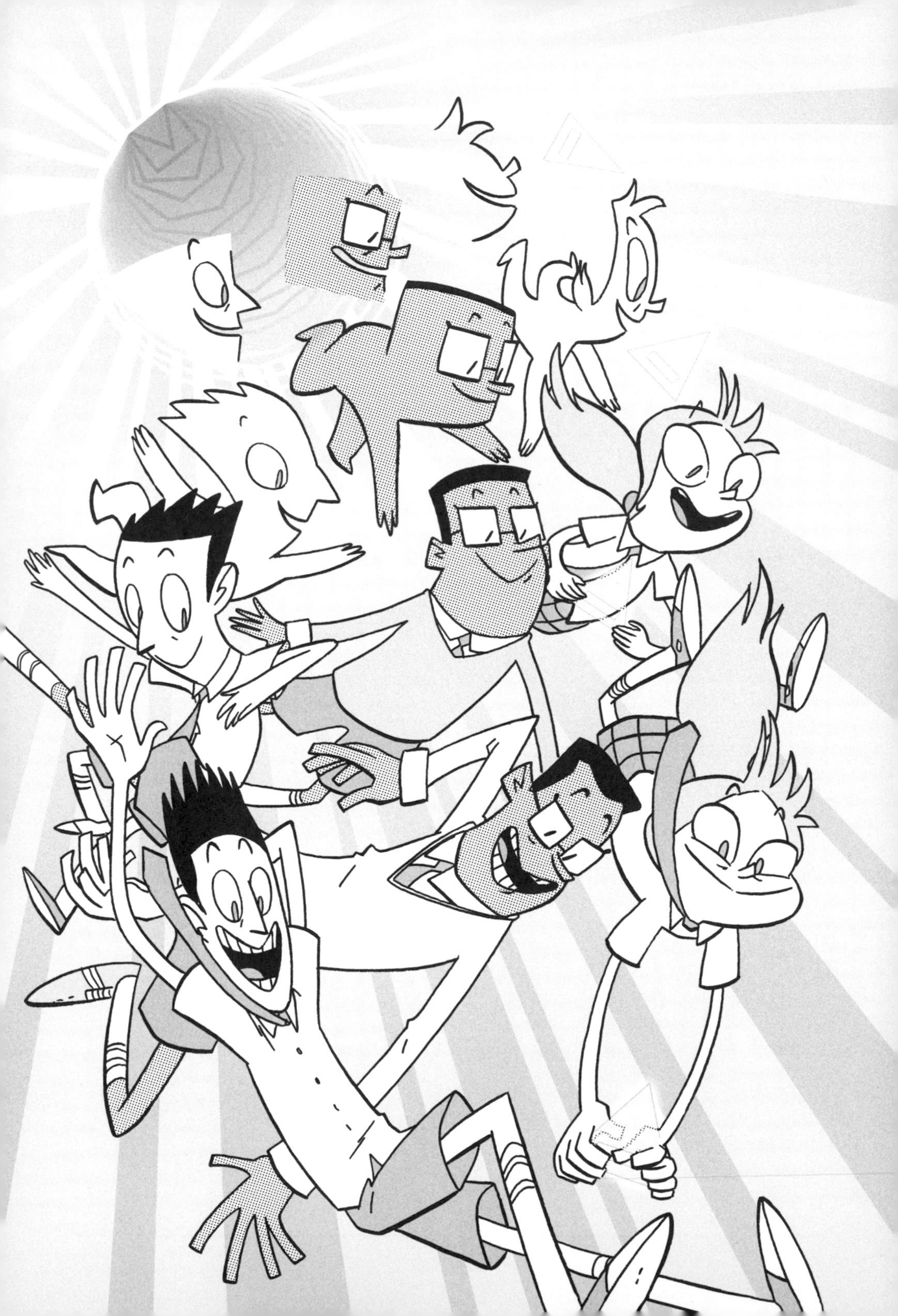

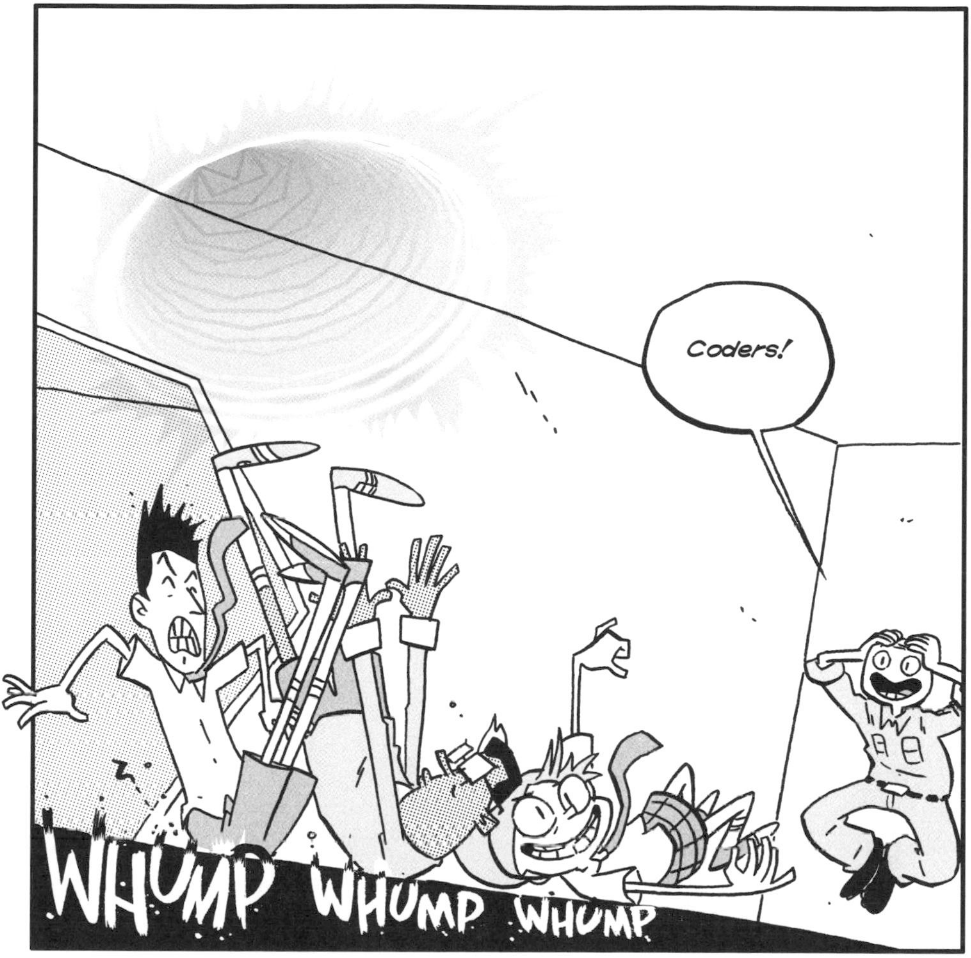
Coders!
WHUMP WHUMP WHUMP

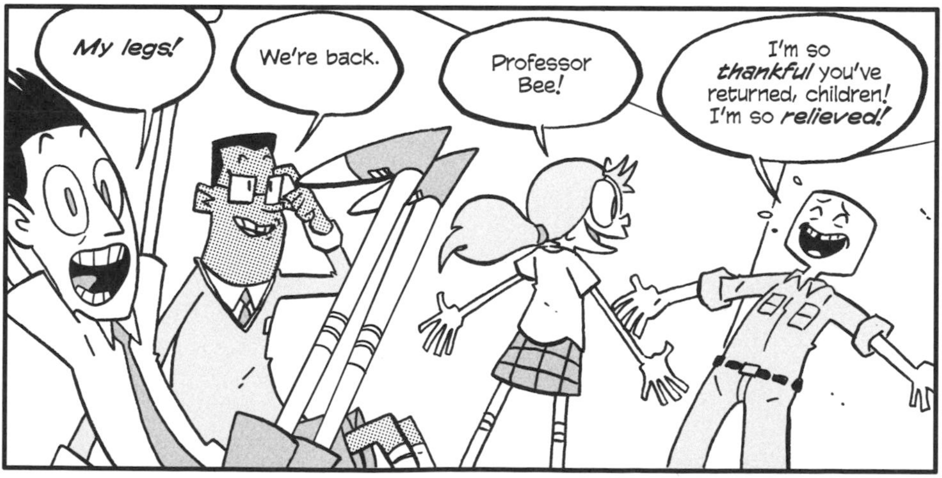
My legs!
We're back.
Professor Bee!
I'm so thankful you've returned, children! I'm so relieved!

40

41

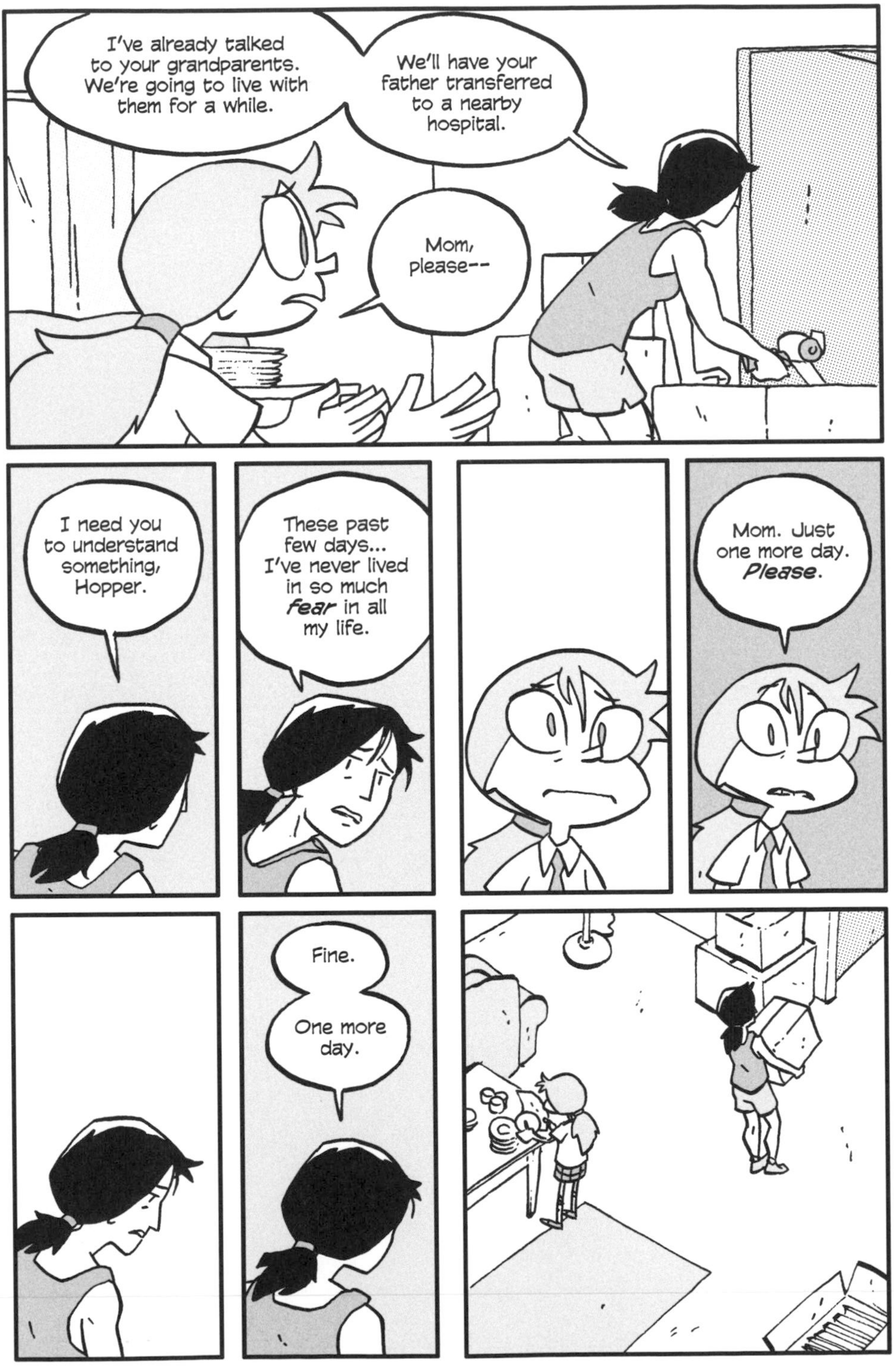
I've already talked to your grandparents. We're going to live with them for a while.
We'll have your father transferred to a nearby hospital.
Mom, please--
I need you to understand something, Hopper.
These past few days... I've never lived in so much *fear* in all my life.
Mom. Just one more day. ***Please***.
Fine.
One more day.

44

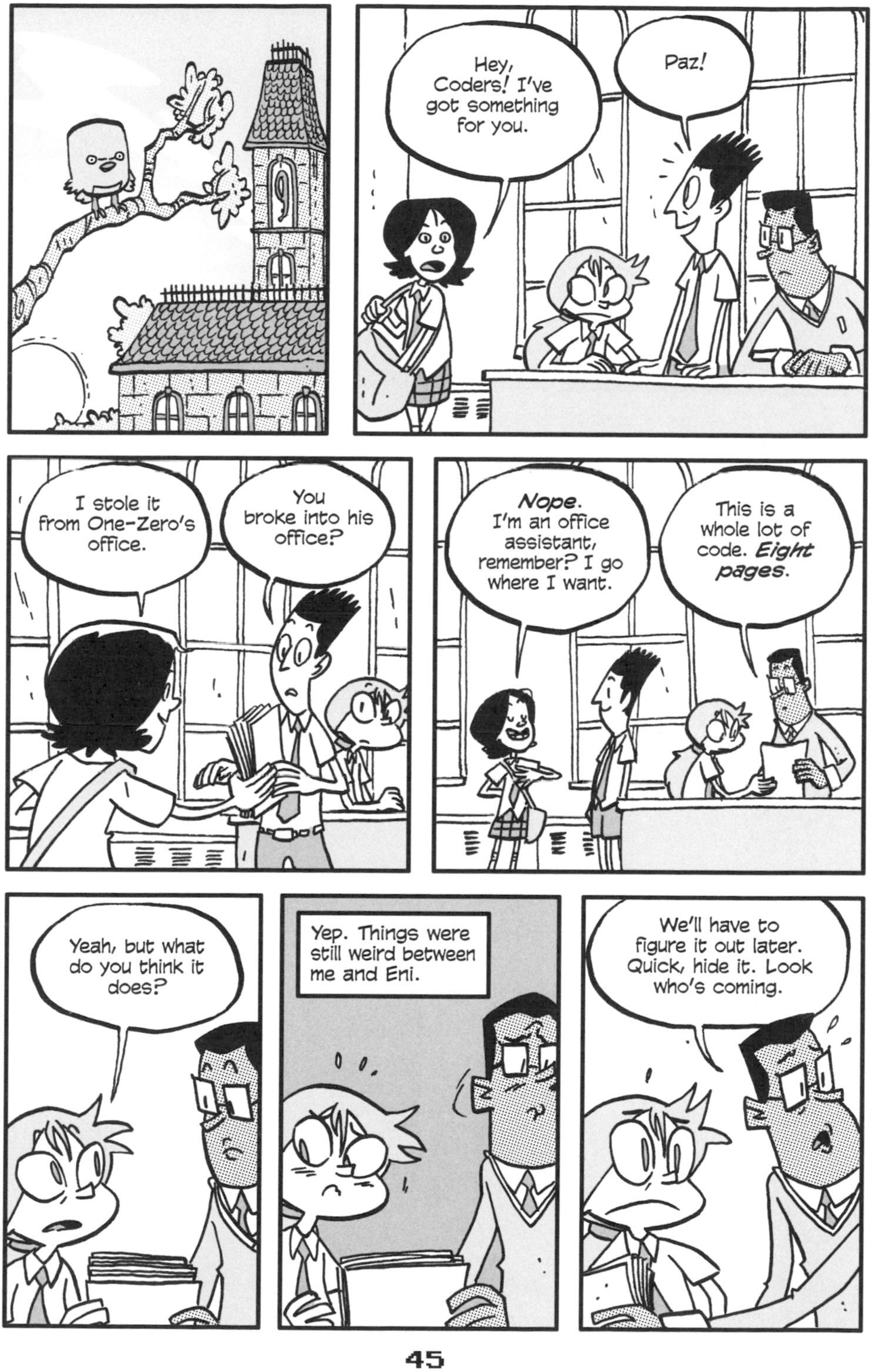
Hey, Coders! I've got something for you.
Paz!
I stole it from One-Zero's office.
You broke into his office?
Nope. I'm an office assistant, remember? I go where I want.
This is a whole lot of code. Eight pages.
Yeah, but what do you think it does?
Yep. Things were still weird between me and Eni.
We'll have to figure it out later. Quick, hide it. Look who's coming.

47

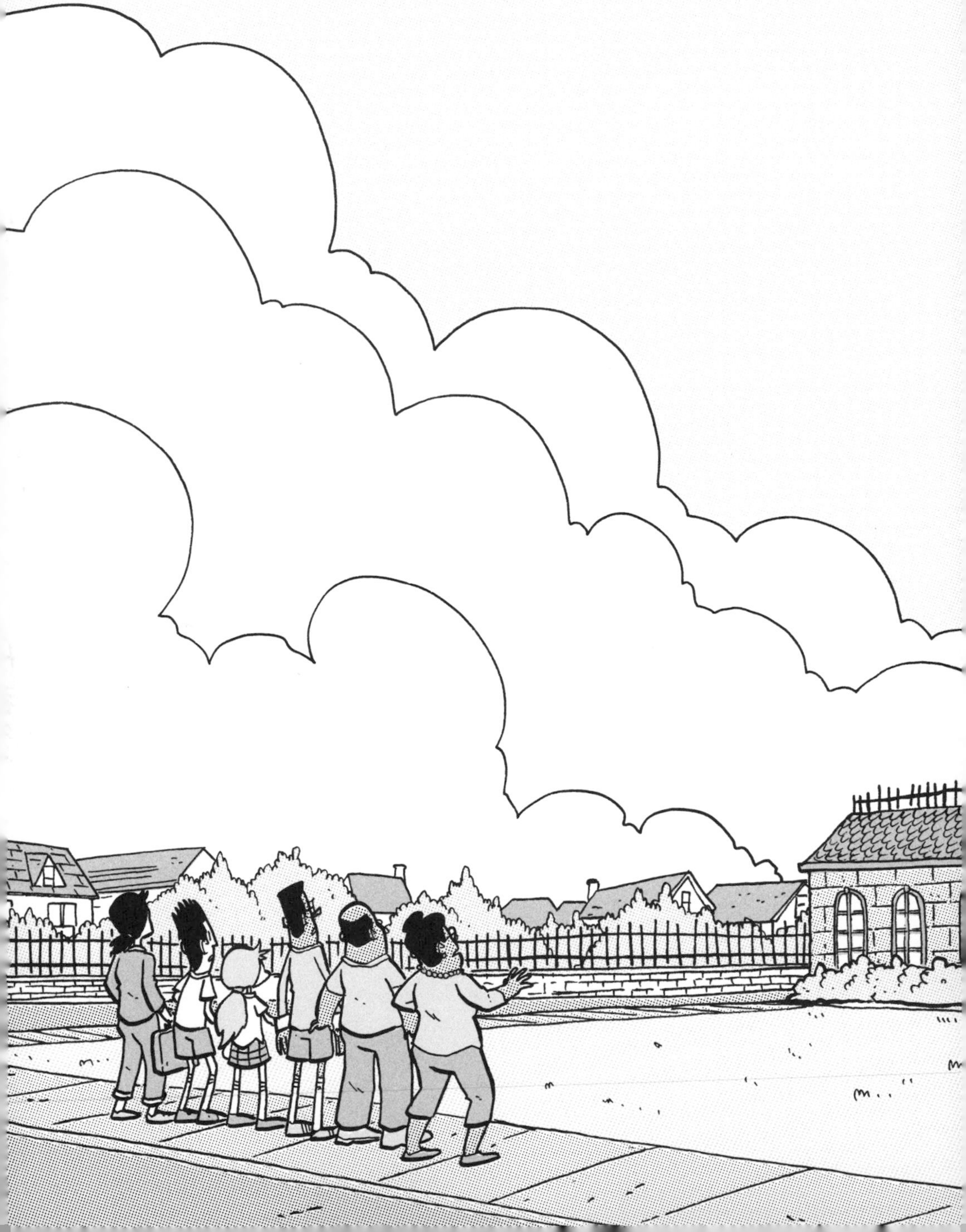

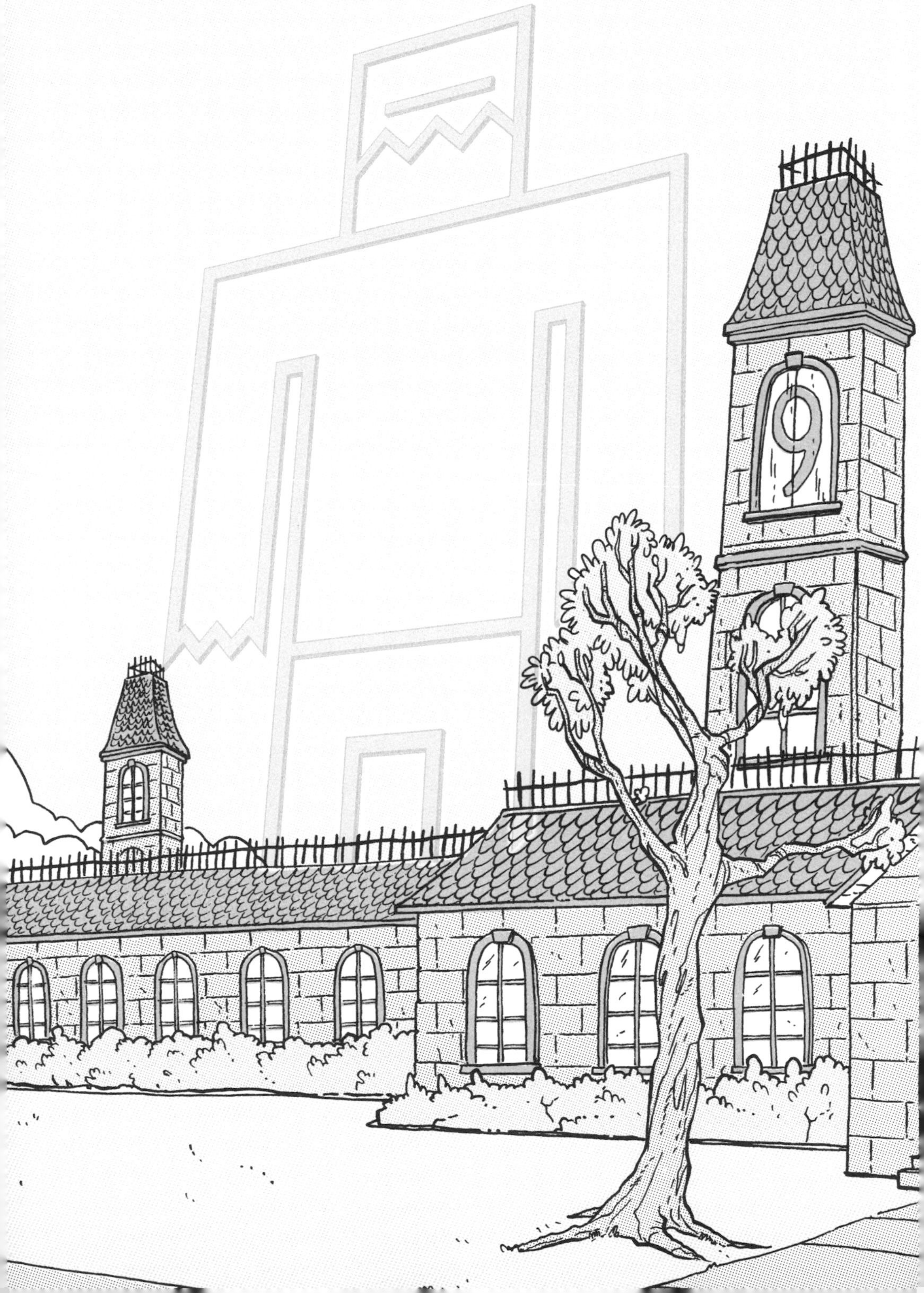
9

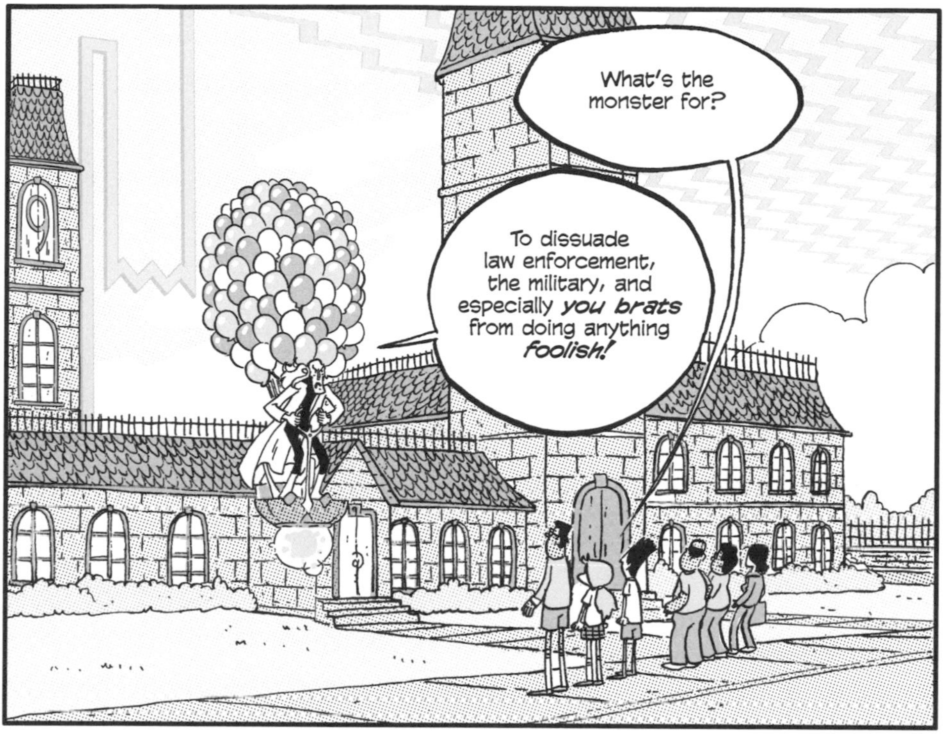
What's the monster for?
To dissuade law enforcement, the military, and especially ***you brats*** from doing anything ***foolish!***

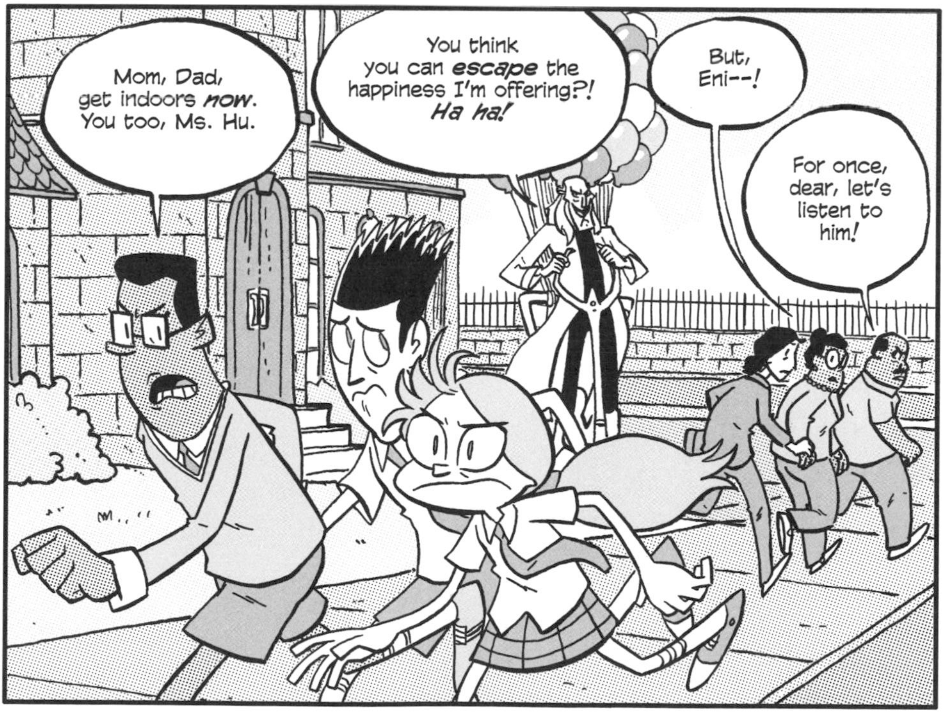
Mom, Dad, get indoors ***now***. You too, Ms. Hu.
You think you can ***escape*** the happiness I'm offering?! ***Ha ha!***
But, Eni--!
For once, dear, let's listen to him!

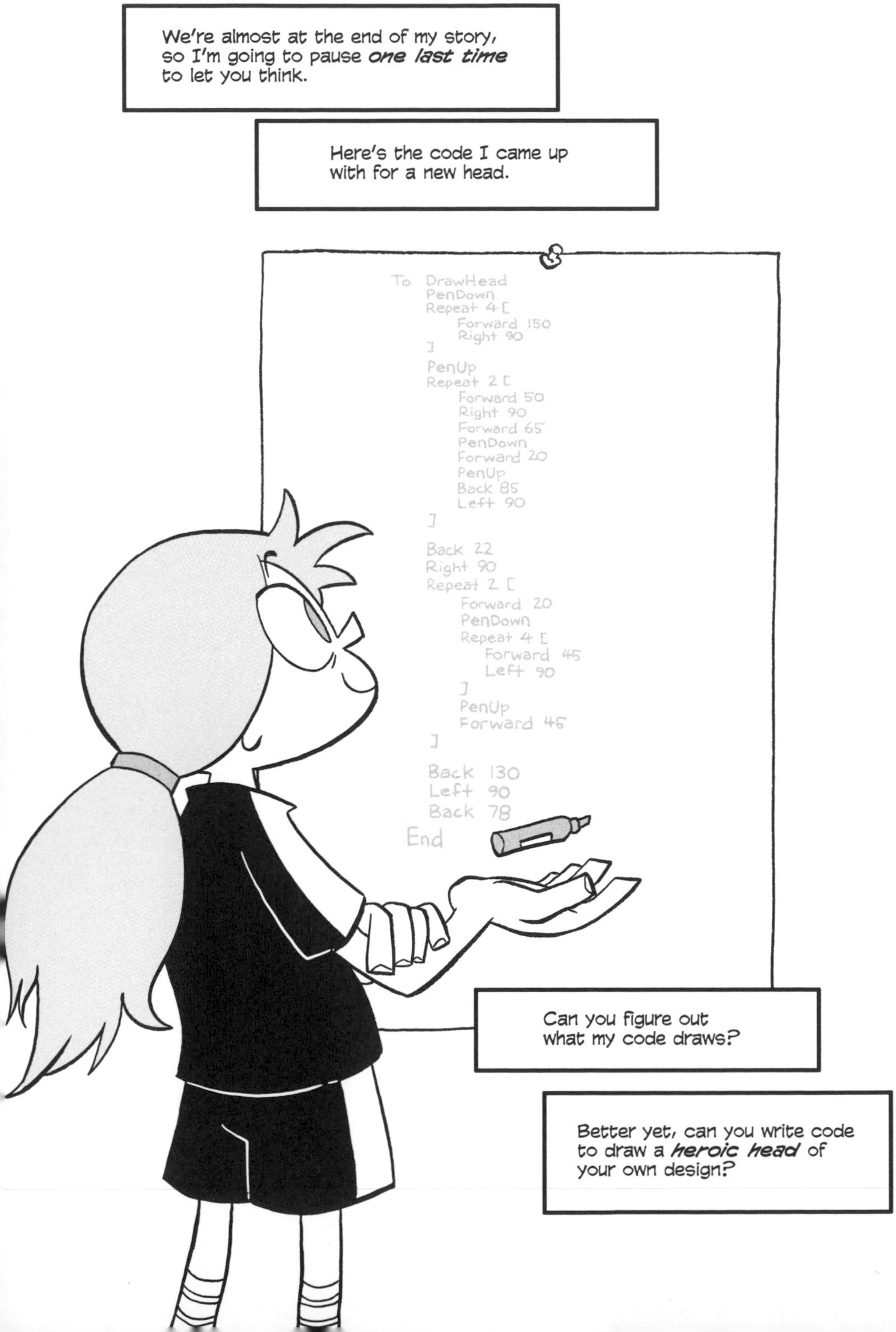
We're almost at the end of my story, so I'm going to pause *one last time* to let you think.
Here's the code I came up with for a new head.
To DrawHead
PenDown
Repeat 4 [
Forward 150
Right 90
]
PenUp
Repeat 2 [
Forward 50
Right 90
Forward 65
PenDown
Forward 20
PenUp
Back 85
Left 90
]
Back 22
Right 90
Repeat 2 [
Forward 20
PenDown
Repeat 4 [
Forward 45
Left 90
]
PenUp
Forward 45
]
Back 130
Left 90
Back 78
End
Can you figure out what my code draws?
Better yet, can you write code to draw a *heroic head* of your own design?

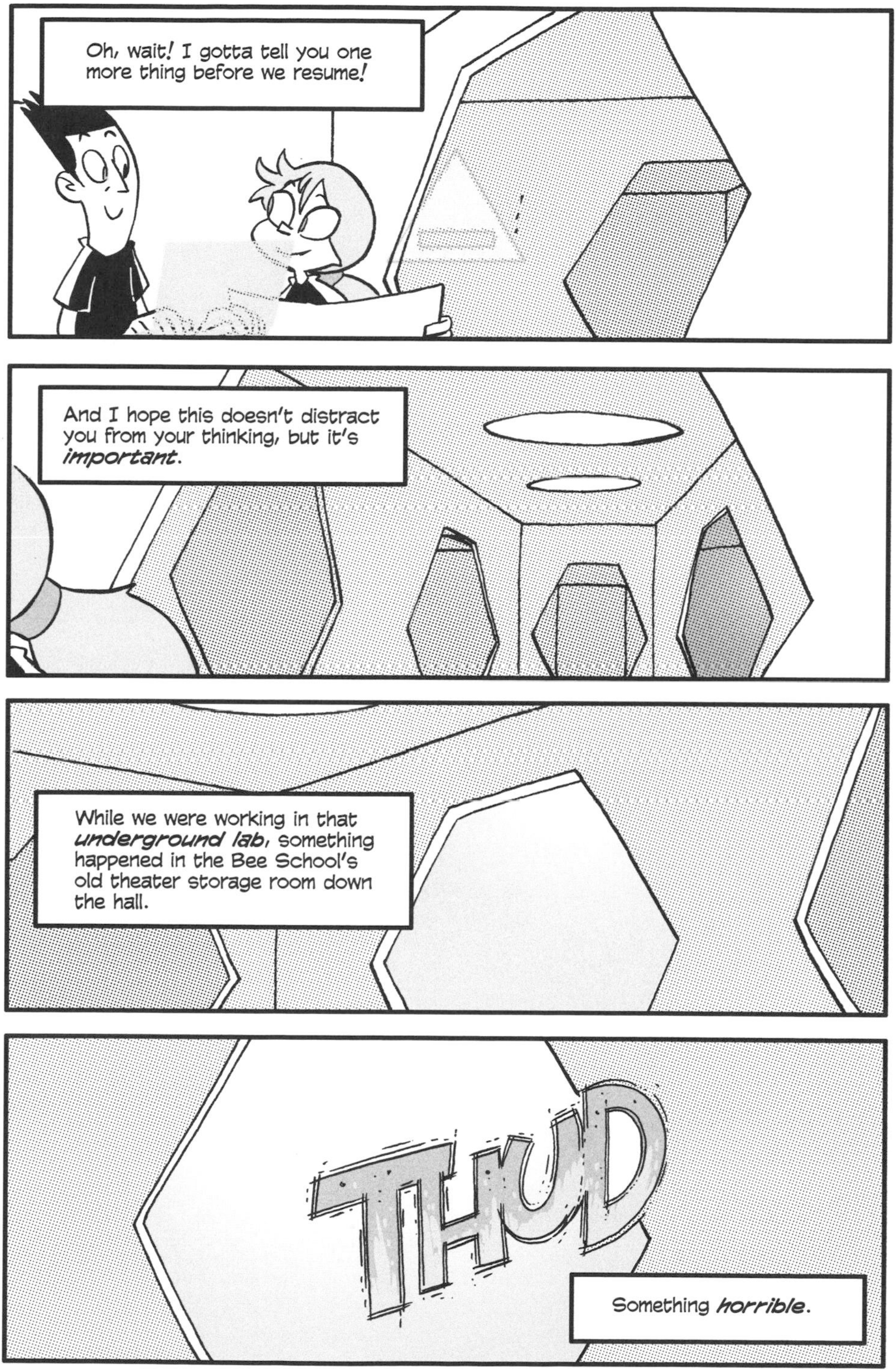
Oh, wait! I gotta tell you one more thing before we resume!
And I hope this doesn't distract you from your thinking, but it's *important*.
While we were working in that *underground lab*, something happened in the Bee School's old theater storage room down the hall.
THUD
Something *horrible*.

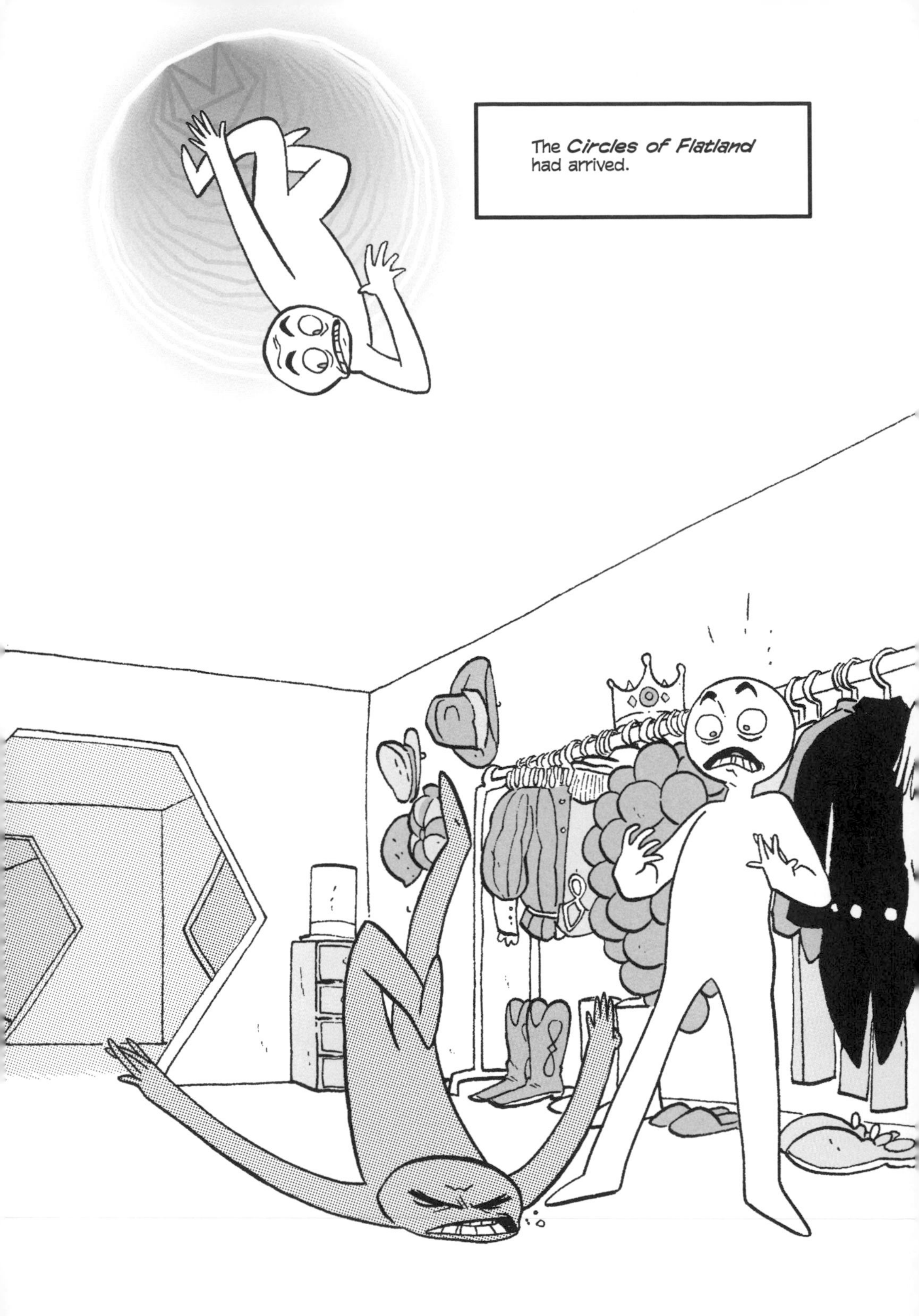
The *Circles of Flatland*
had arrived.

Chapter

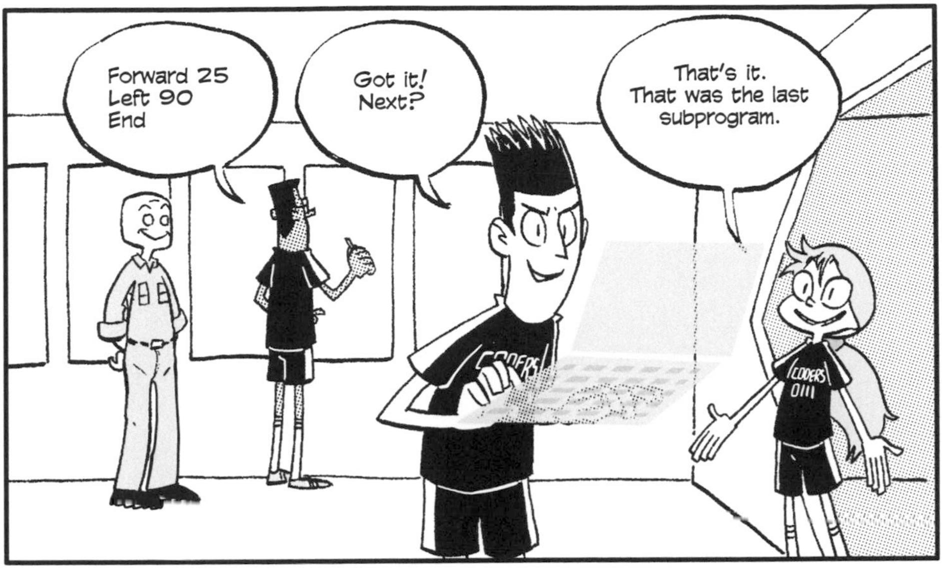
Forward 25
Left 90
End
Got it! Next?
That's it. That was the last subprogram.

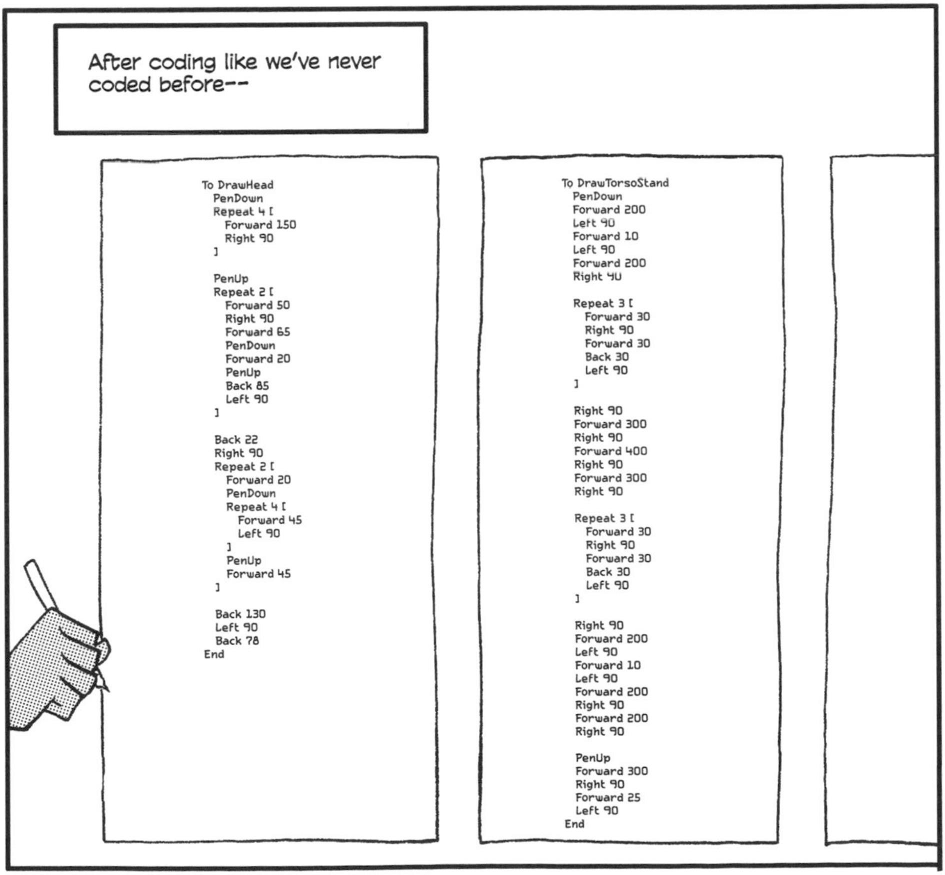
After coding like we've never coded before--
To DrawHead
PenDown
Repeat 4 [
Forward 150
Right 90
]
PenUp
Repeat 2 [
Forward 50
Right 90
Forward 65
PenDown
Forward 20
PenUp
Back 85
Left 90
]
Back 22
Right 90
Repeat 2 [
Forward 20
PenDown
Repeat 4 [
Forward 45
Left 90
]
PenUp
Forward 45
]
Back 130
Left 90
Back 78
End
To DrawTorsoStand
PenDown
Forward 200
Left 90
Forward 10
Left 90
Forward 200
Right 90
Repeat 3 [
Forward 30
Right 90
Forward 30
Back 30
Left 90
]
Right 90
Forward 300
Right 90
Forward 400
Right 90
Forward 300
Right 90
Repeat 3 [
Forward 30
Right 90
Forward 30
Back 30
Left 90
]
Right 90
Forward 200
Left 90
Forward 10
Left 90
Forward 200
Right 90
Forward 200
Right 90
PenUp
Forward 300
Right 90
Forward 25
Left 90
End

--we created six subprograms.

That's one more than One-Zero had because Josh added one called *DrawCrouchingLegs*.

```
To DrawTorsoPunch
  PenDown
  Forward 200
  Left 90
  Forward 10
  Left 90
  Forward 200
  Right 90
  Repeat 3 [
    Forward 30
    Right 90
    Forward 30
    Back 30
    Left 90
  ]
  Right 90
  Forward 300
  Right 90
  Forward 525
  Right 90
  Repeat 3 [
    Forward 30
    Right 90
    Forward 30
    Back 30
    Left 90
  ]
  Right 90
  Forward 225
  Left 90
  Forward 210
  Right 90
  Forward 200
  Right 90
  PenUp
  Forward 300
  Right 90
  Forward 25
  Left 90
End
```

```
To DrawTorsoBlock
  PenDown
  Forward 200
  Left 90
  Forward 10
  Left 90
  Forward 200
  Right 90
  Repeat 3 [
    Forward 30
    Right 90
    Forward 30
    Back 30
    Left 90
  ]
  Right 90
  Forward 300
  Right 90
  Forward 350
  Left 90
  Forward 150
  Right 90
  Repeat 3 [
    Forward 30
    Right 90
    Forward 30
    Back 30
    Left 90
  ]
  Right 90
  Forward 240
  Right 90
  Forward 140
  Left 90
  Forward 210
  Right 90
  Forward 200
  Right 90
  PenUp
  Forward 300
  Right 90
  Forward 25
  Left 90
End
```

```
To DrawLegs
  PenDown
  Right 45
  Forward 35
  Left 45
  Forward 225
  Right 90
  Forward 200
  Right 90
  Forward 225
  Left 45
  Forward 35
  Right 135
  Forward 100
  Right 90
  Forward 175
  Left 90
  Forward 50
  Left 90
  Forward 175
  Right 90
  Forward 100
  Right 90
  PenUp
  Forward 250
  Right 90
  Forward 25
  Left 90
End
```

```
To DrawCrouchingLegs
  PenDown
  Right 45
  Forward 35
  Left 45
  Forward 150
  Right 90
  Forward 400
  Right 90
  Forward 150
  Left 45
  Forward 35
  Right 135
  Forward 100
  Right 90
  Forward 100
  Left 90
  Forward 250
  Left 90
  Forward 100
  Right 90
  Forward 100
  Right 90
  PenUp
  Forward 175
  Right 90
  Forward 125
  Left 90
End
```

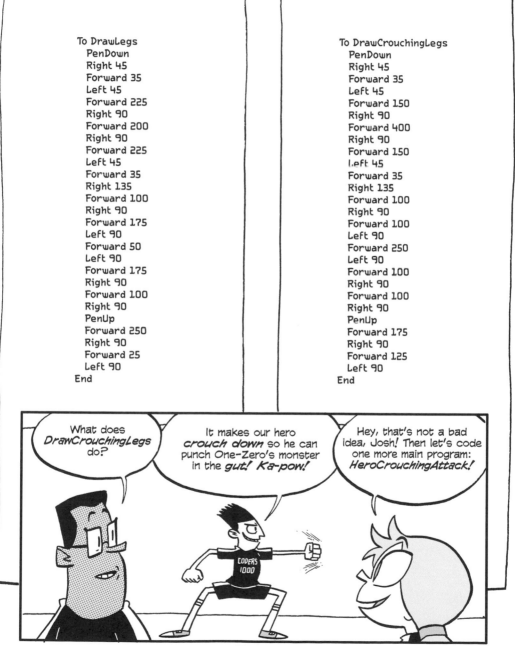

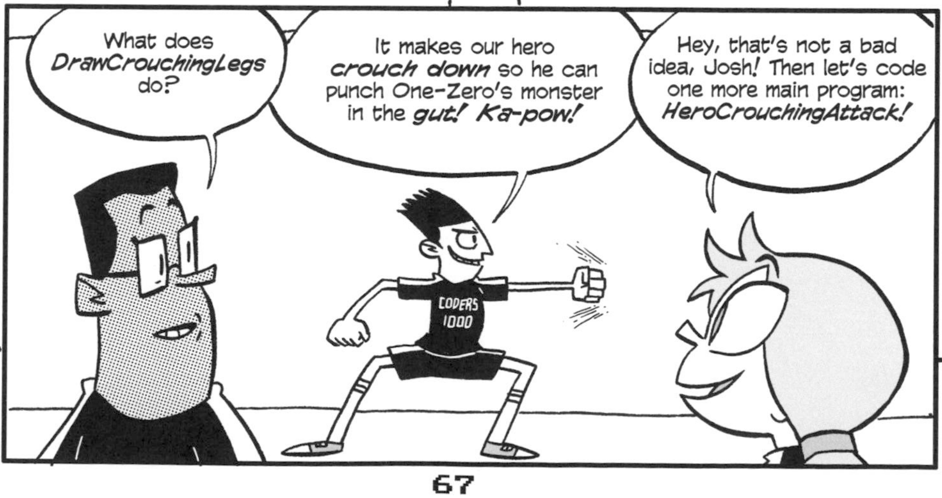
What does *DrawCrouchingLegs* do?
It makes our hero ***crouch down*** so he can punch One-Zero's monster in the ***gut! Ka-pow!***
Hey, that's not a bad idea, Josh! Then let's code one more main program: *HeroCrouchingAttack!*
CODERS 1000

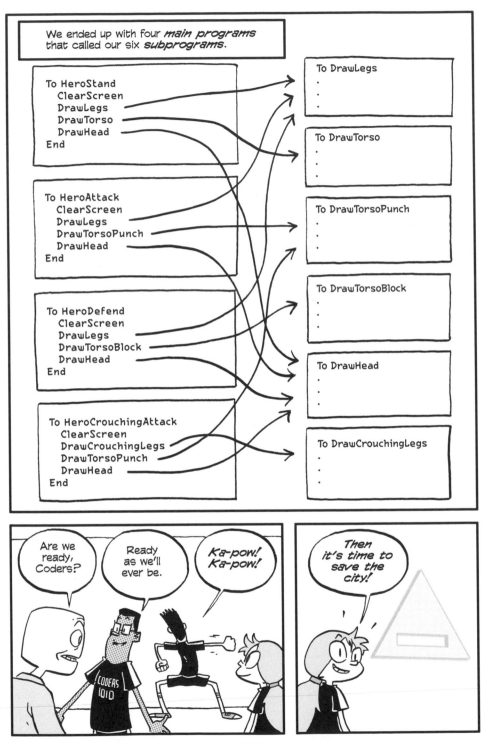

We ended up with four **main programs** that called our six **subprograms**.

```
To HeroStand
    ClearScreen
    DrawLegs
    DrawTorso
    DrawHead
End
```

```
To HeroAttack
    ClearScreen
    DrawLegs
    DrawTorsoPunch
    DrawHead
End
```

```
To HeroDefend
    ClearScreen
    DrawLegs
    DrawTorsoBlock
    DrawHead
End
```

```
To HeroCrouchingAttack
    ClearScreen
    DrawCrouchingLegs
    DrawTorsoPunch
    DrawHead
End
```

```
To DrawLegs
    .
    .
    .
```

```
To DrawTorso
    .
    .
    .
```

```
To DrawTorsoPunch
    .
    .
    .
```

```
To DrawTorsoBlock
    .
    .
    .
```

```
To DrawHead
    .
    .
    .
```

```
To DrawCrouchingLegs
    .
    .
    .
```

Are we ready, Coders?

Ready as we'll ever be.

Ka-pow! Ka-pow!

Then it's time to save the city!

CODERS 1010

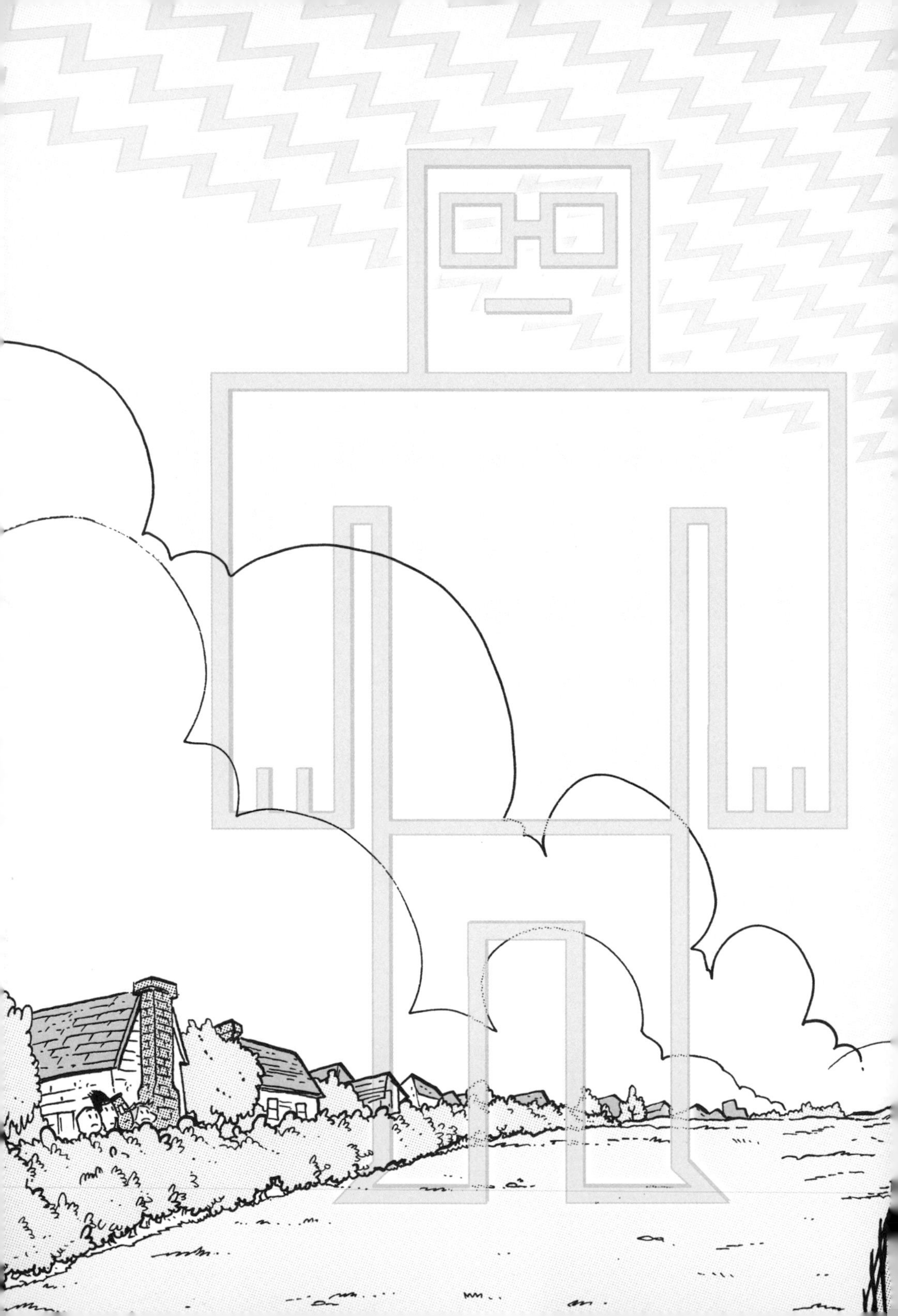

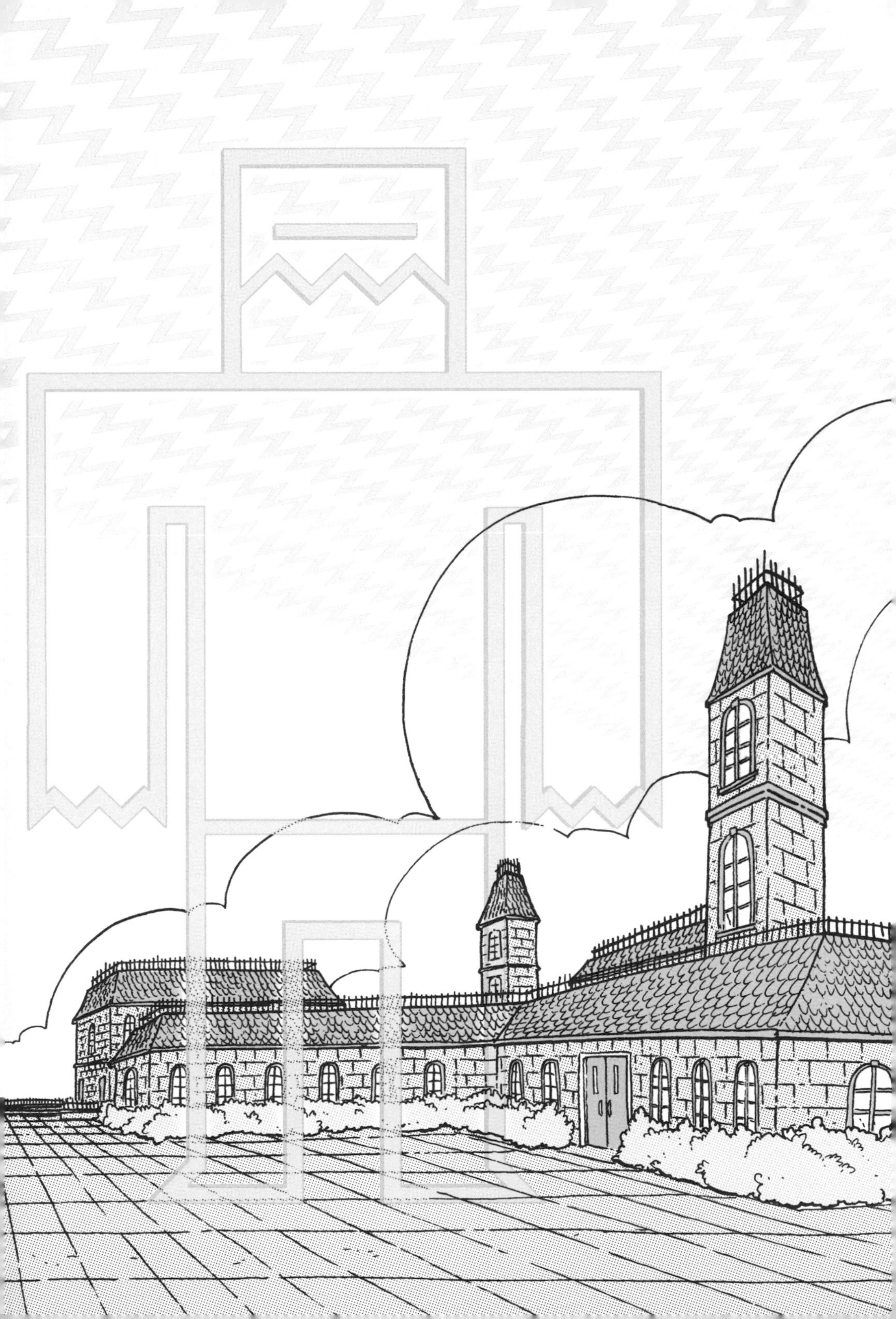

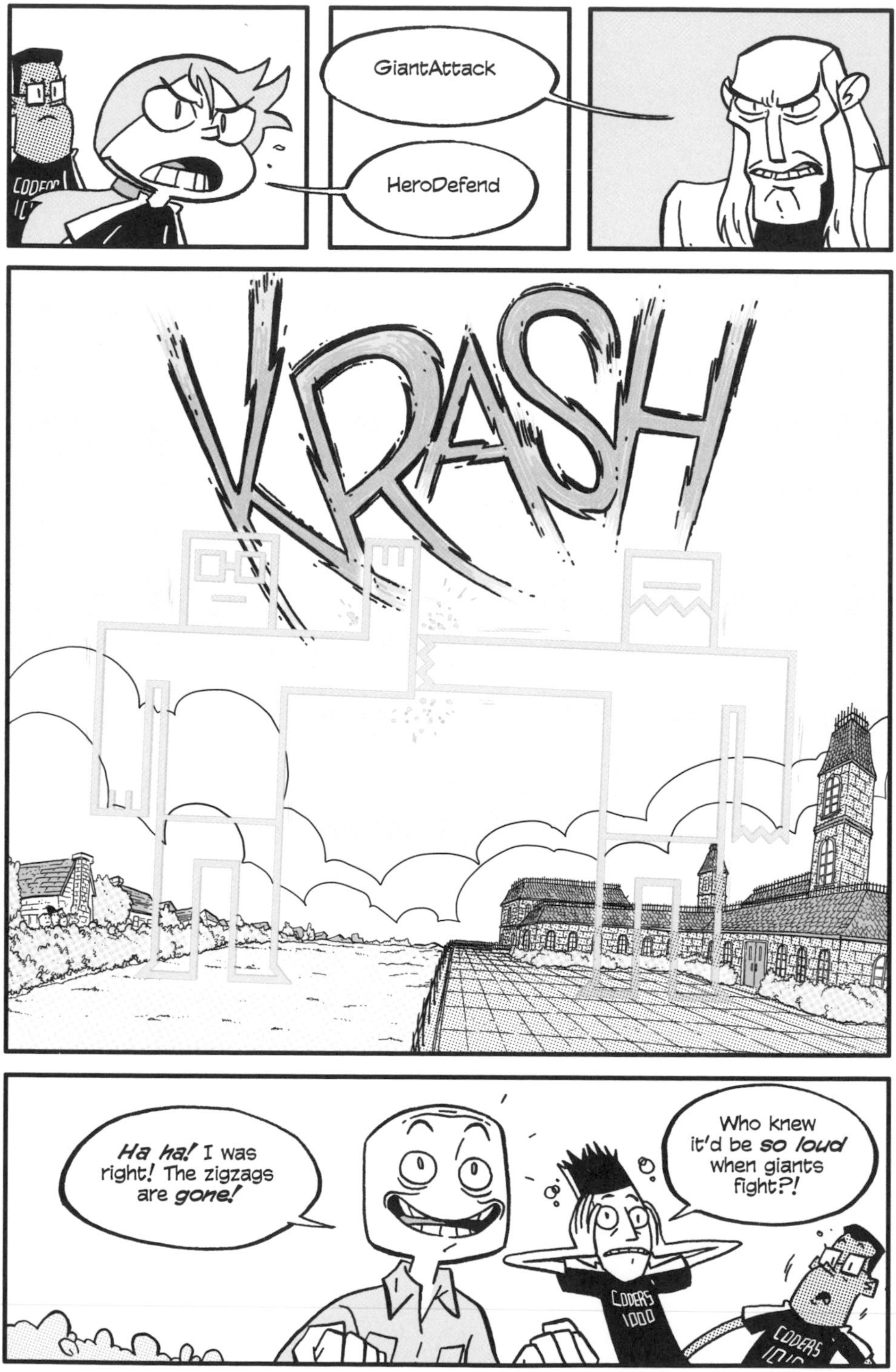
CODERS 1010
GiantAttack
HeroDefend
KRASH
Ha ha! I was right! The zigzags are gone!
Who knew it'd be so loud when giants fight?!
CODERS 1000
CODERS 1010

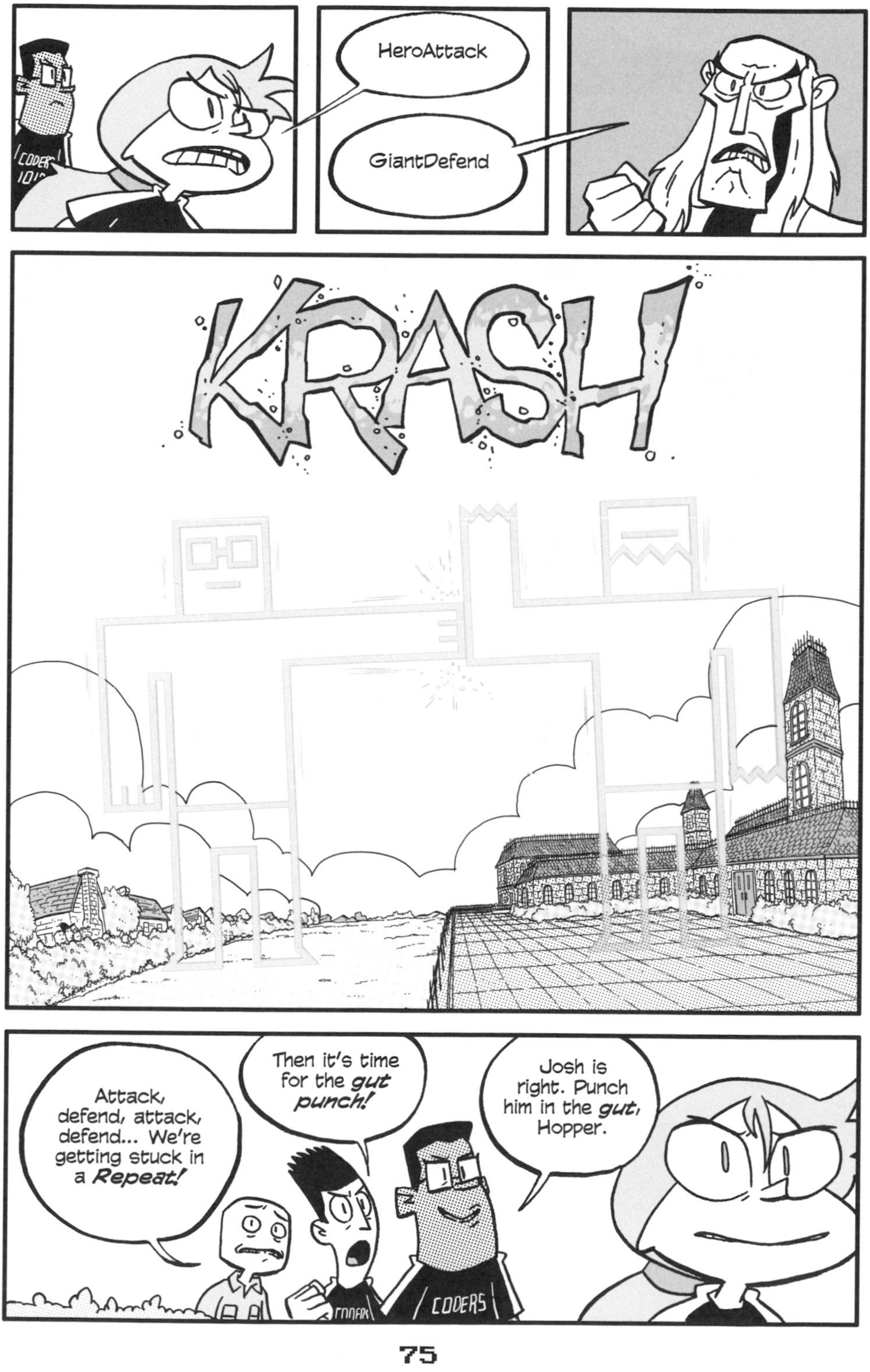
CODERS
HeroAttack
GiantDefend
KRASH
Attack, defend, attack, defend... We're getting stuck in a *Repeat!*
Then it's time for the *gut punch!*
Josh is right. Punch him in the *gut*, Hopper.
CODERS

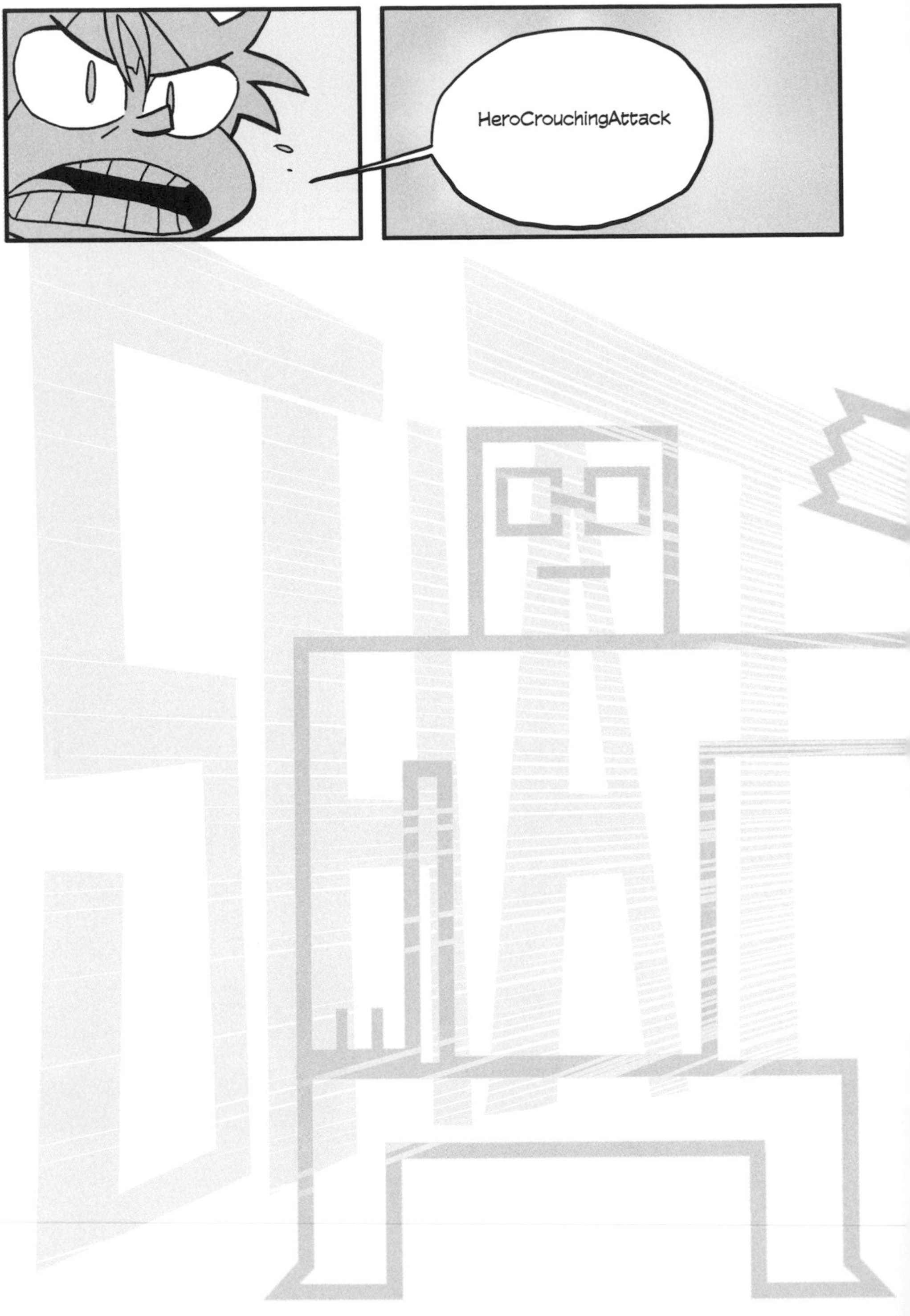
HeroCrouchingAttack

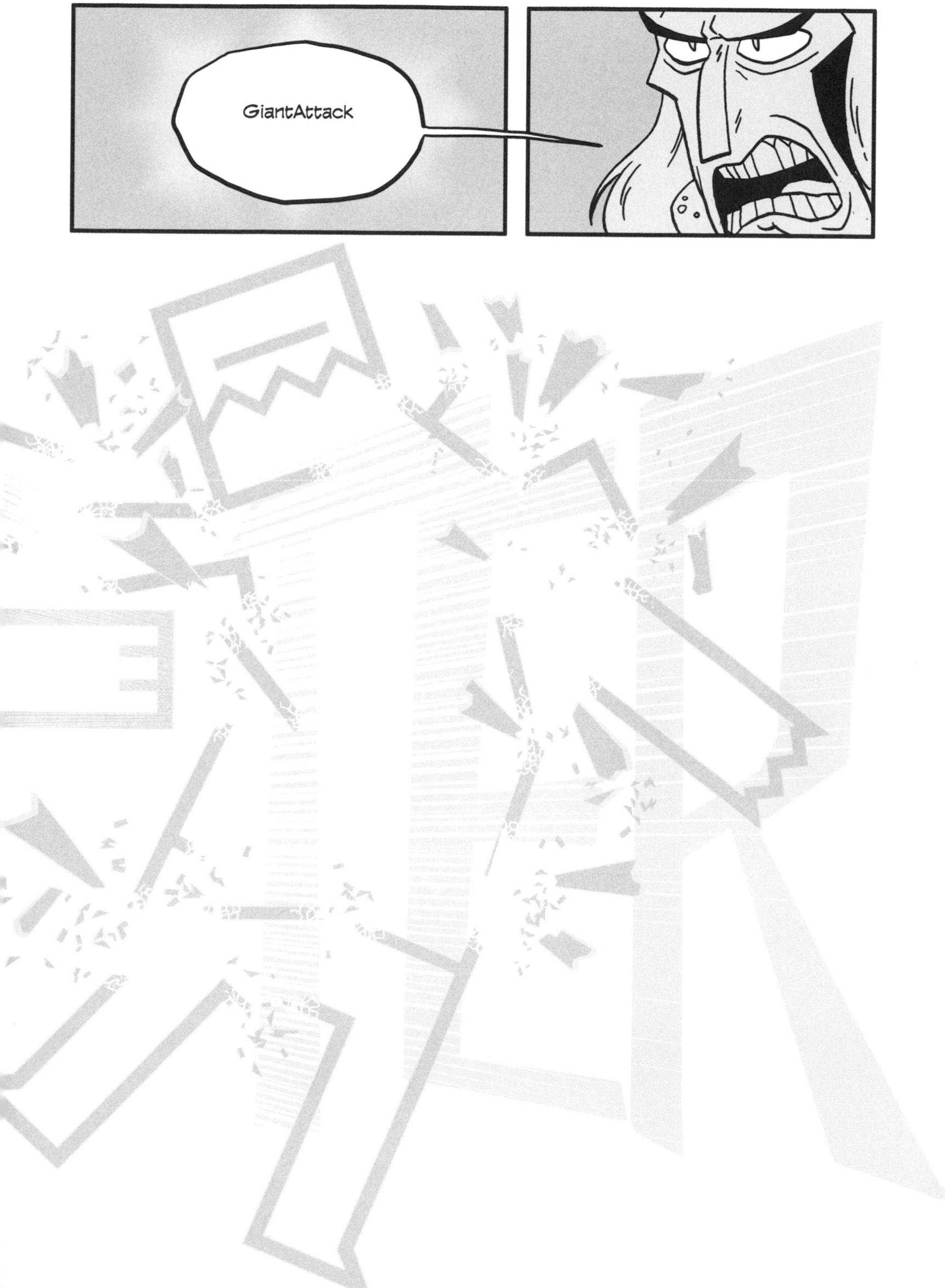
GiantAttack

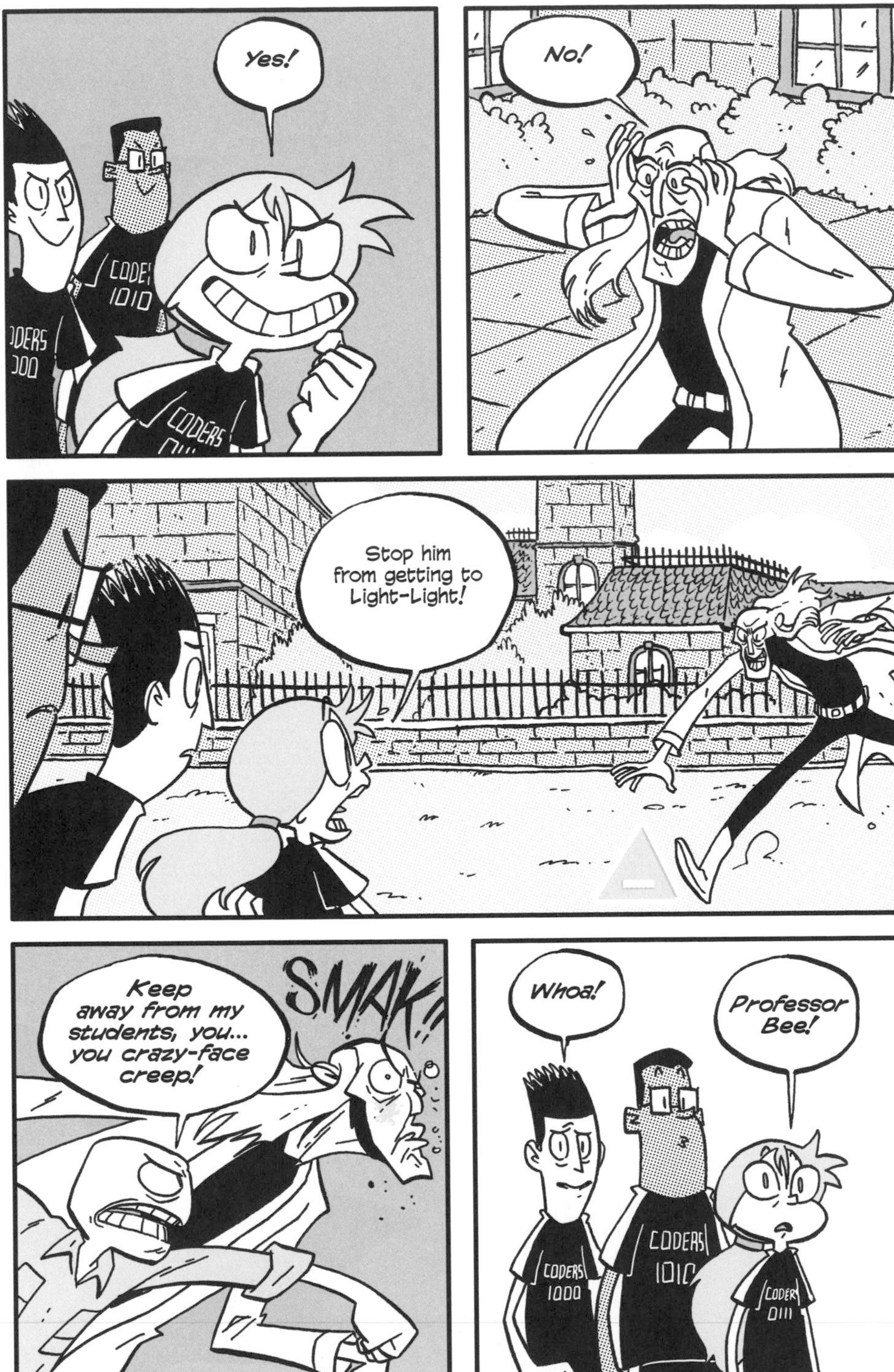
Yes!
CODERS 1010
No!
Stop him from getting to Light-Light!
Keep away from my students, you... you crazy-face creep!
SMAK!!
Whoa!
Professor Bee!
CODERS 1000
CODERS 1010
CODERS 0111

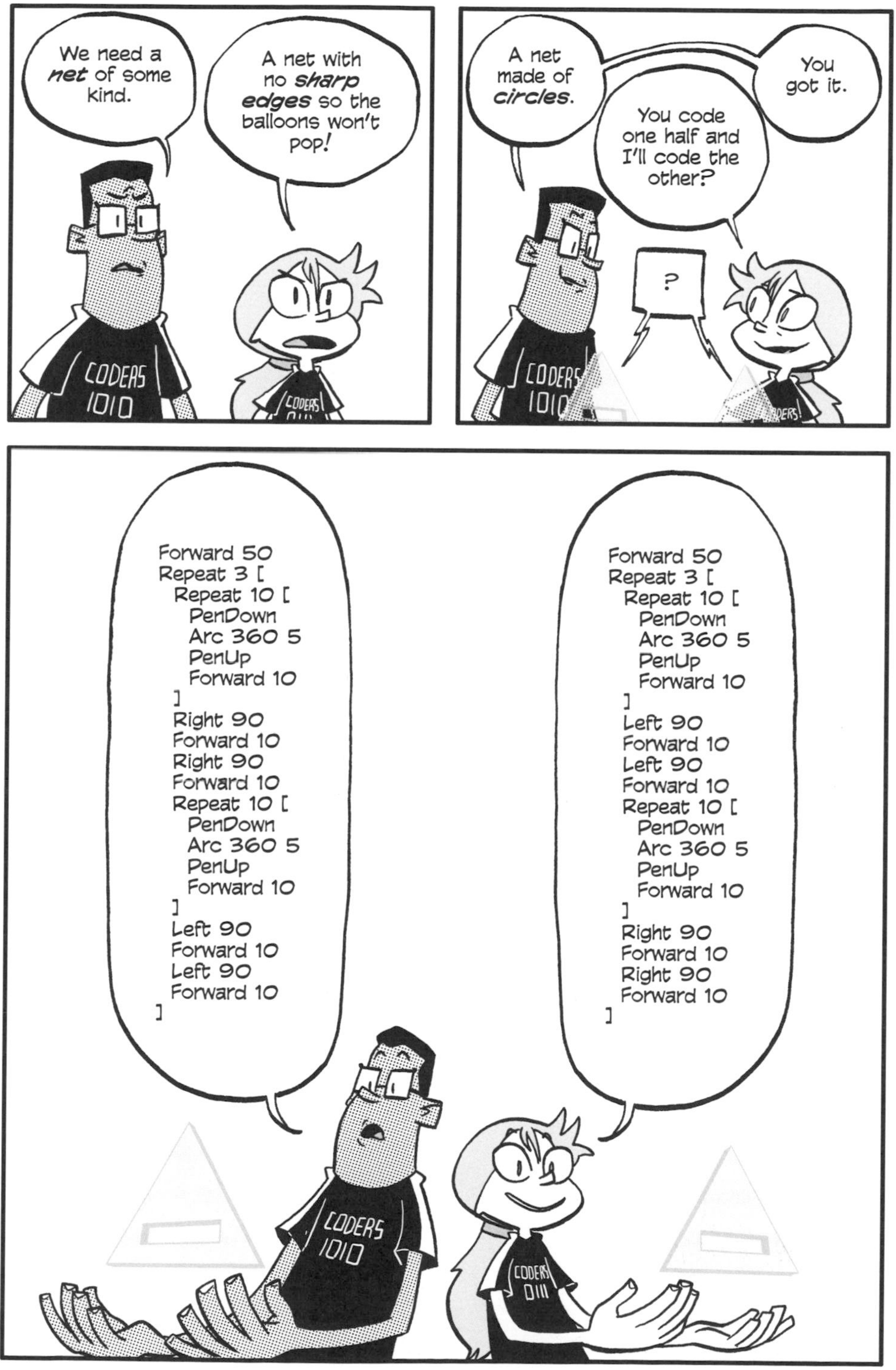
We need a *net* of some kind.
A net with no *sharp edges* so the balloons won't pop!
A net made of *circles*.
You code one half and I'll code the other?
You got it.
?
Forward 50
Repeat 3 [
Repeat 10 [
PenDown
Arc 360 5
PenUp
Forward 10
]
Right 90
Forward 10
Right 90
Forward 10
Repeat 10 [
PenDown
Arc 360 5
PenUp
Forward 10
]
Left 90
Forward 10
Left 90
Forward 10
]
Forward 50
Repeat 3 [
Repeat 10 [
PenDown
Arc 360 5
PenUp
Forward 10
]
Left 90
Forward 10
Left 90
Forward 10
Repeat 10 [
PenDown
Arc 360 5
PenUp
Forward 10
]
Right 90
Forward 10
Right 90
Forward 10
]

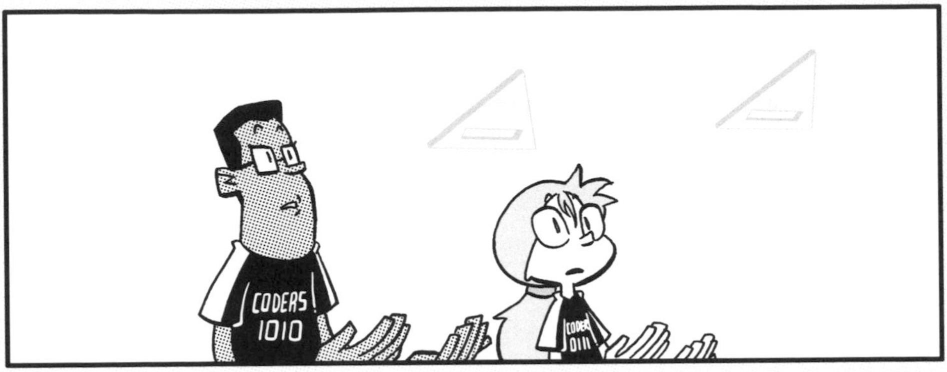
CODERS
1010
CODERS
0111
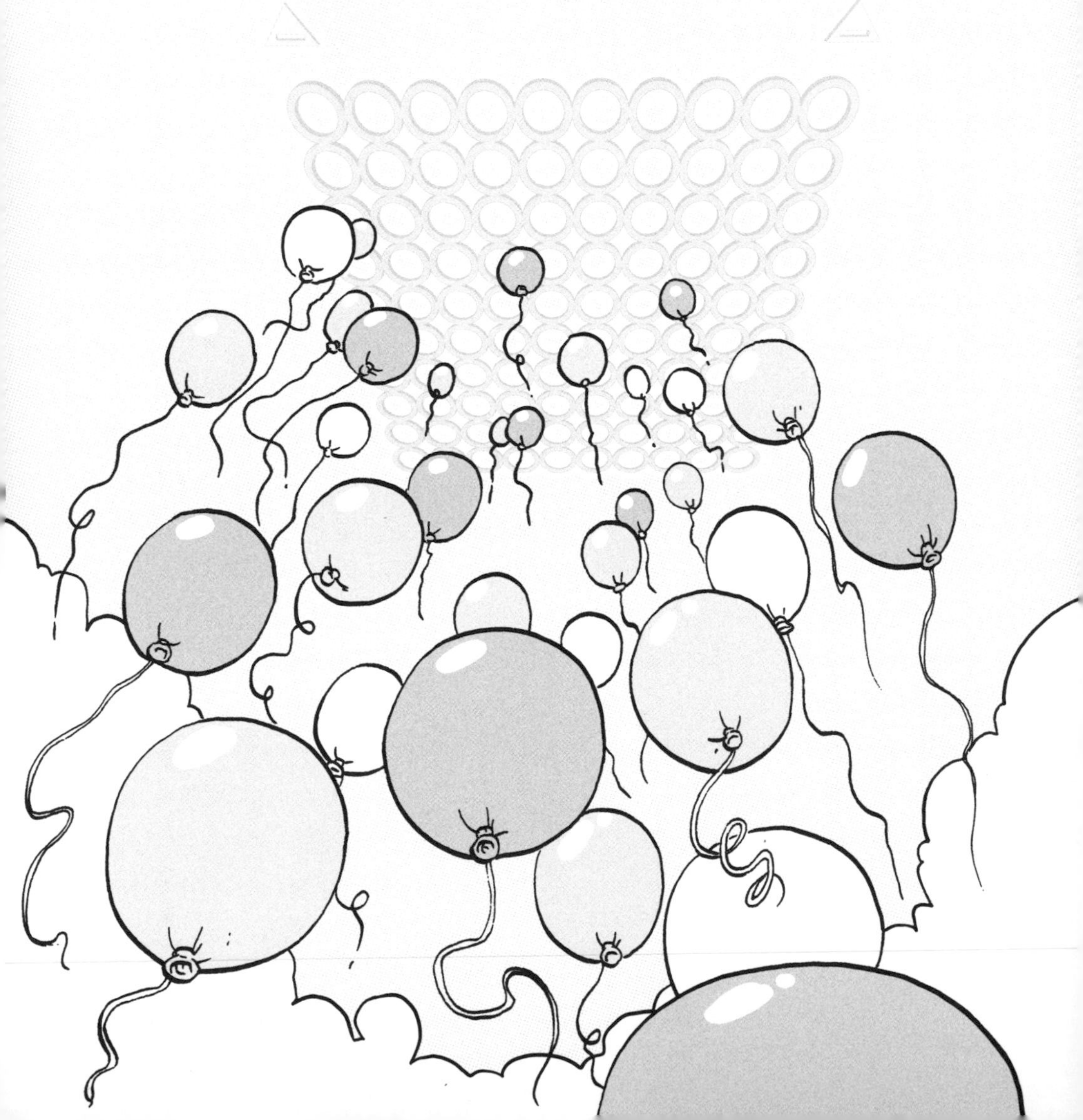

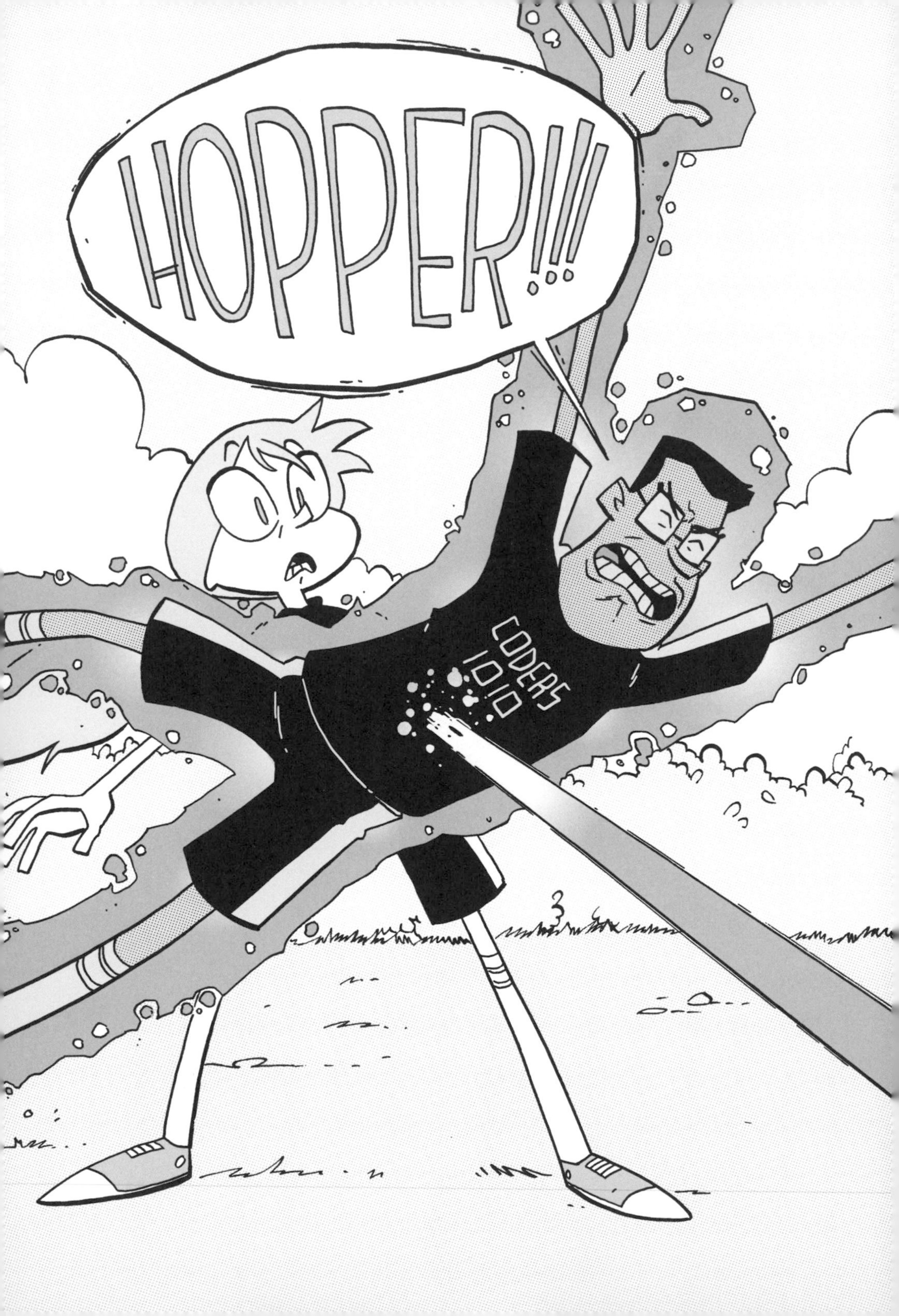
HOPPER!!!
CODERS
10 10

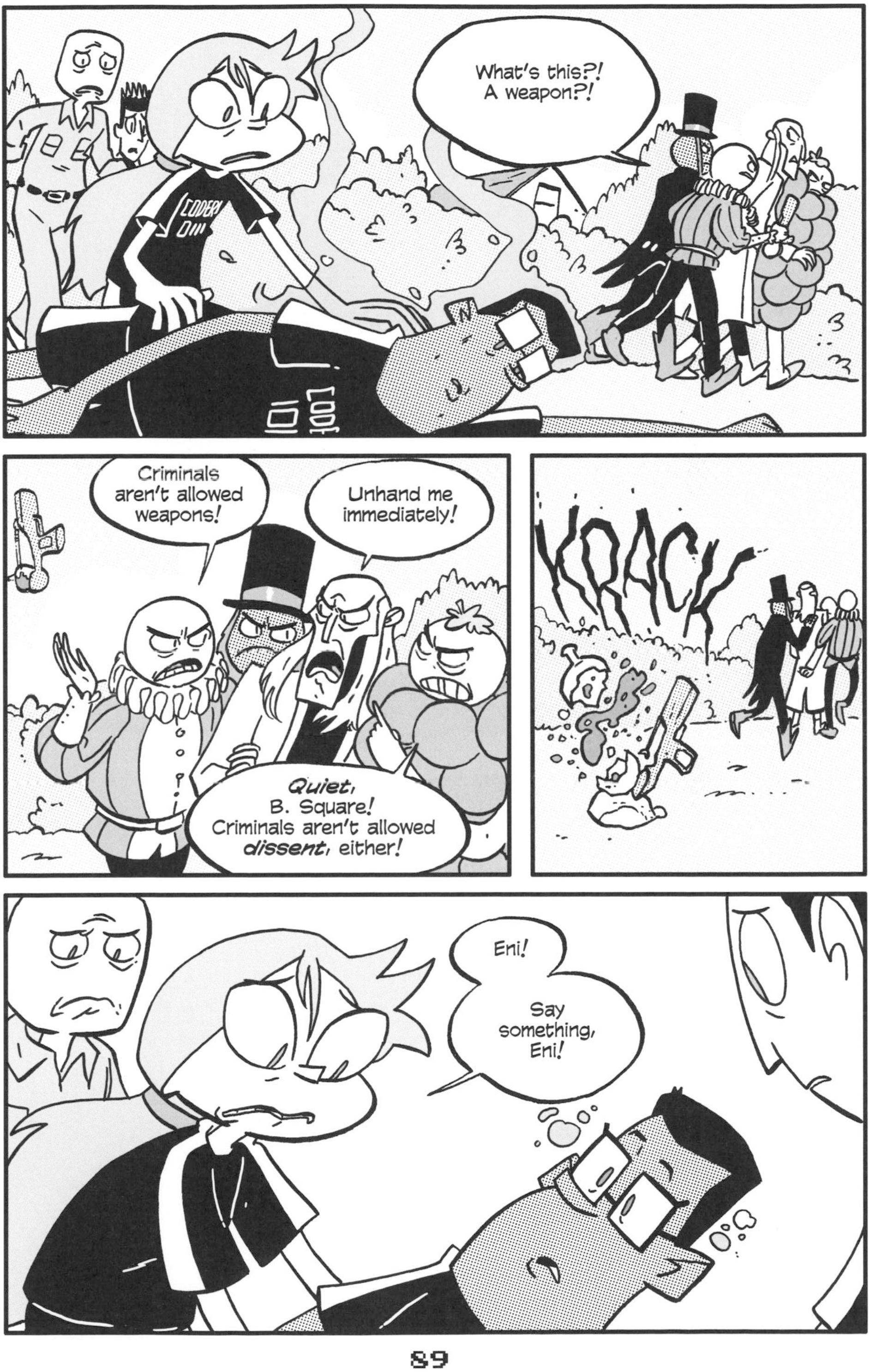
What's this?! A weapon?!
CODER DIII
Criminals aren't allowed weapons!
Unhand me immediately!
Quiet, B. Square! Criminals aren't allowed *dissent,* either!
KRACK
Eni!
Say something, Eni!

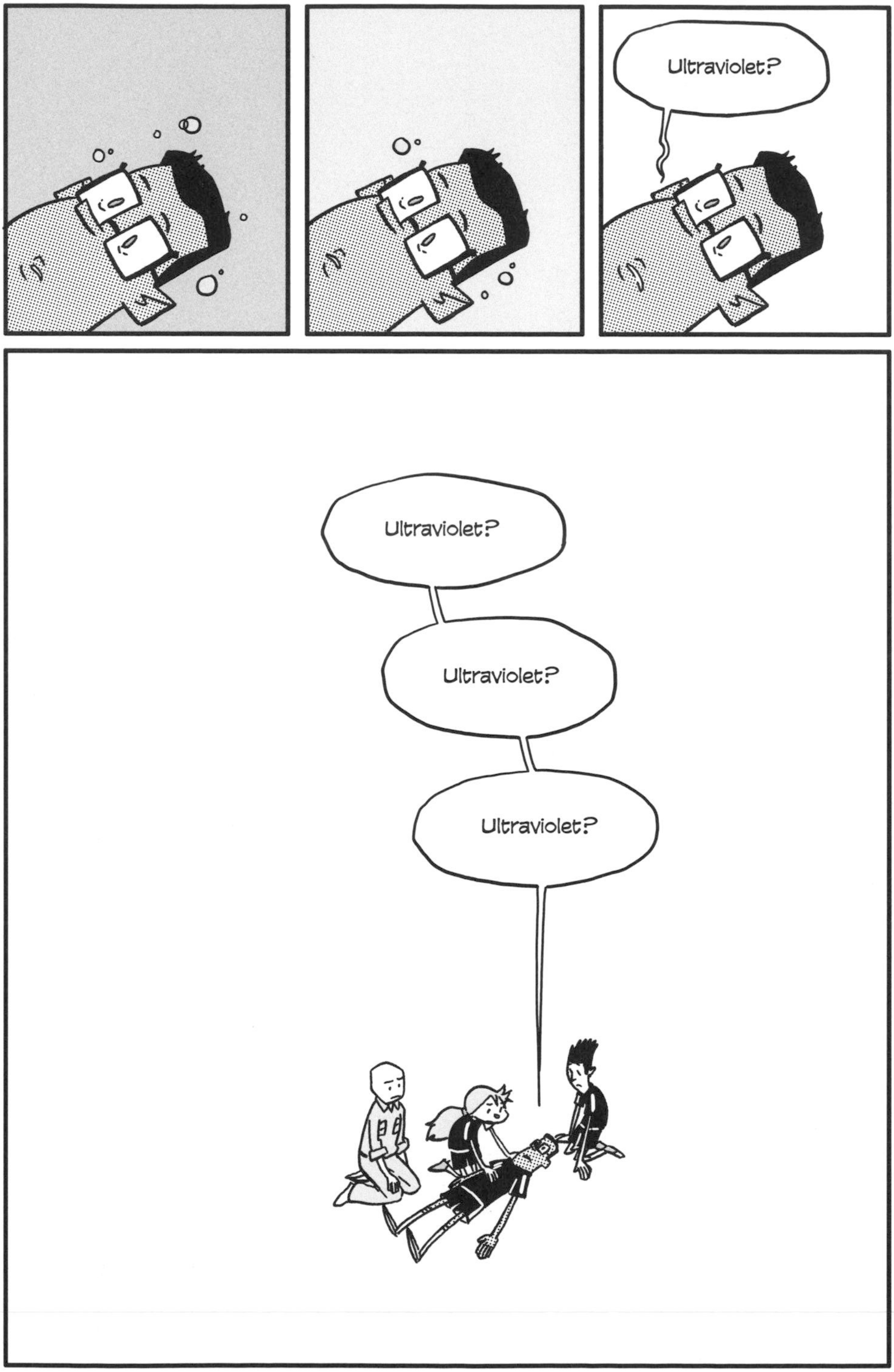
Ultraviolet?
Ultraviolet?
Ultraviolet?
Ultraviolet?

That was three weeks ago.

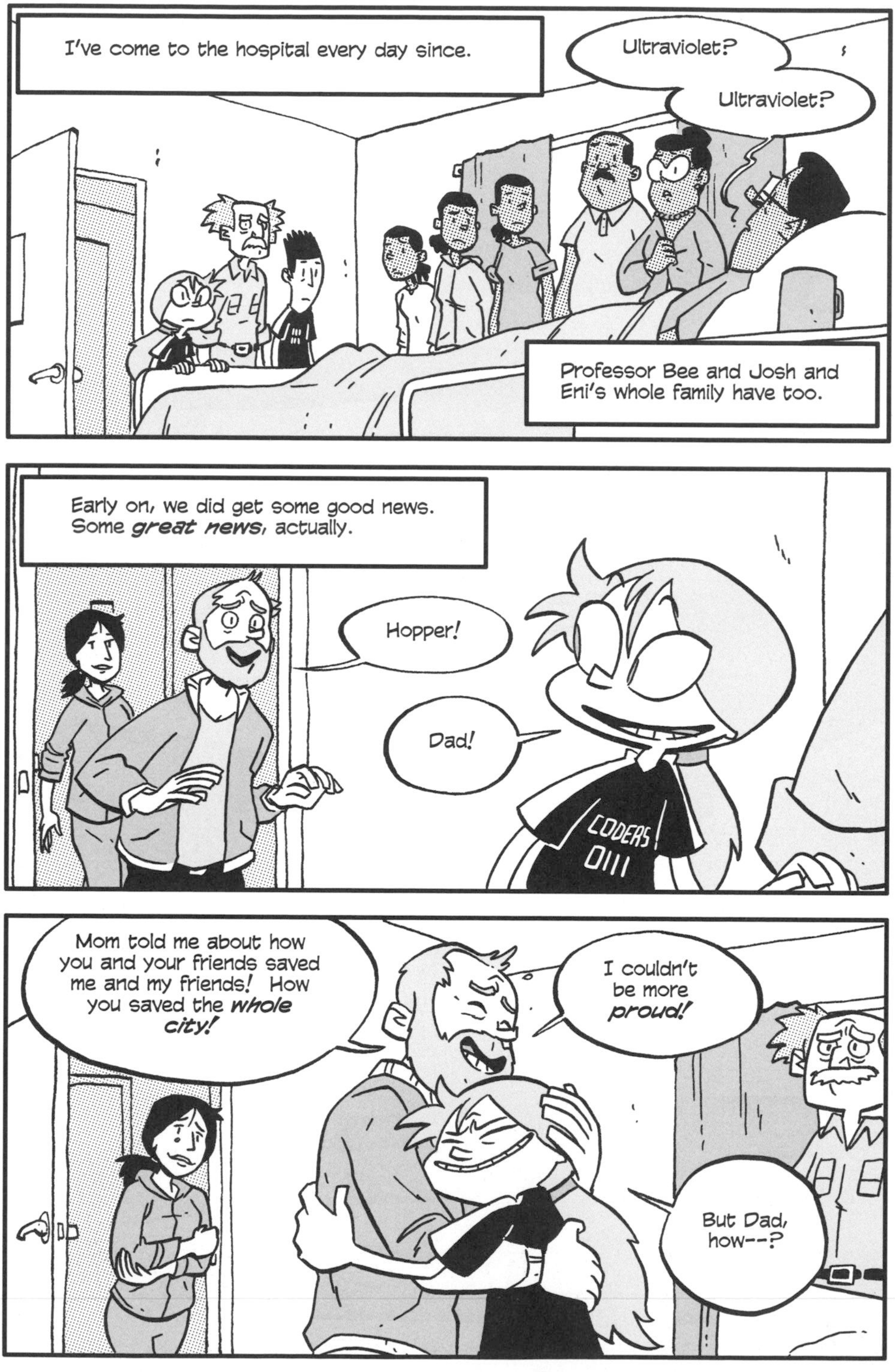
I've come to the hospital every day since.
Ultraviolet?
Ultraviolet?
Professor Bee and Josh and Eni's whole family have too.
Early on, we did get some good news. Some *great news*, actually.
Hopper!
Dad!
CODERS 0111
Mom told me about how you and your friends saved me and my friends! How you saved the *whole city!*
I couldn't be more *proud!*
But Dad, how--?

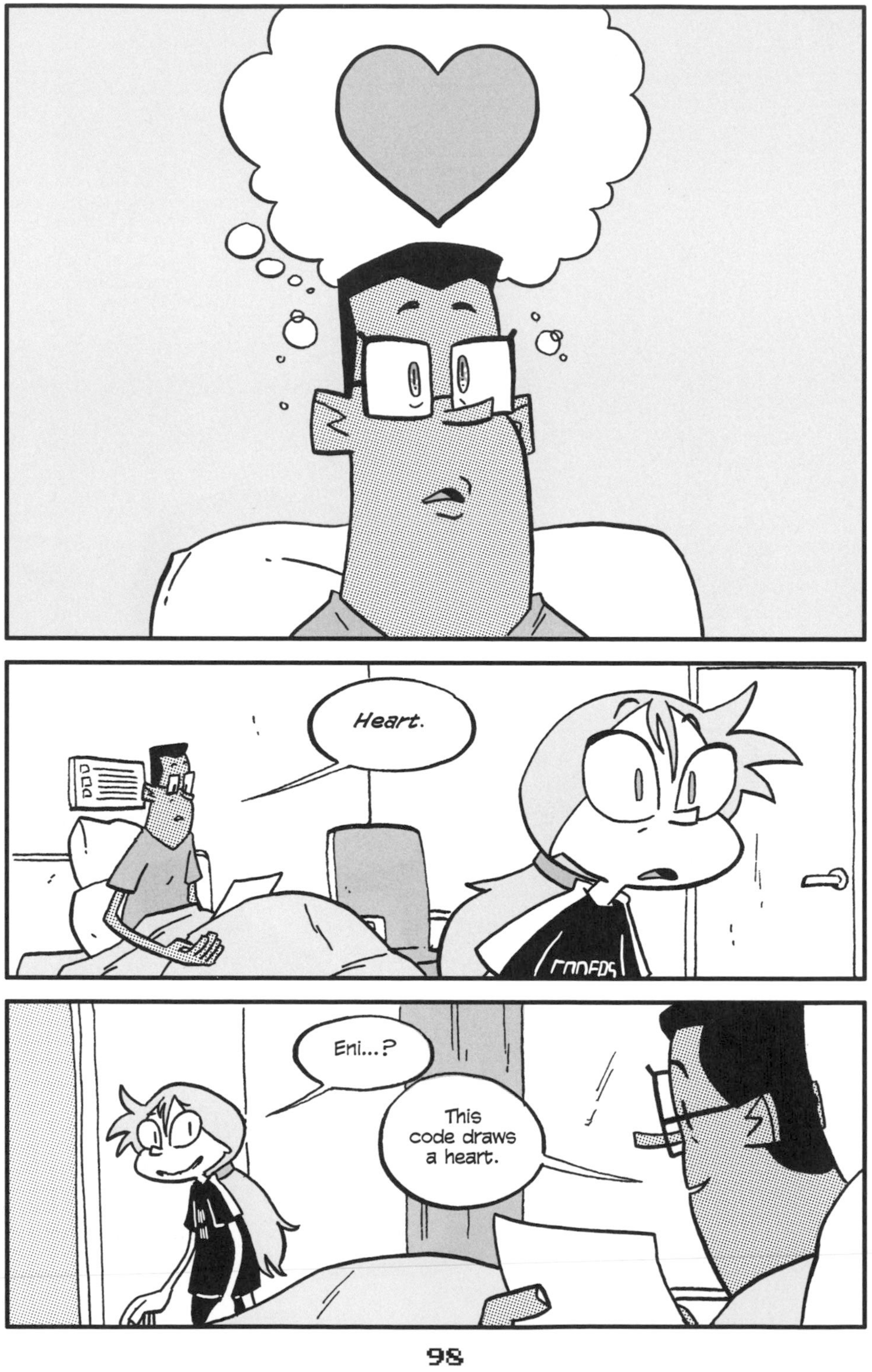
Heart.
Eni...?
This code draws a heart.

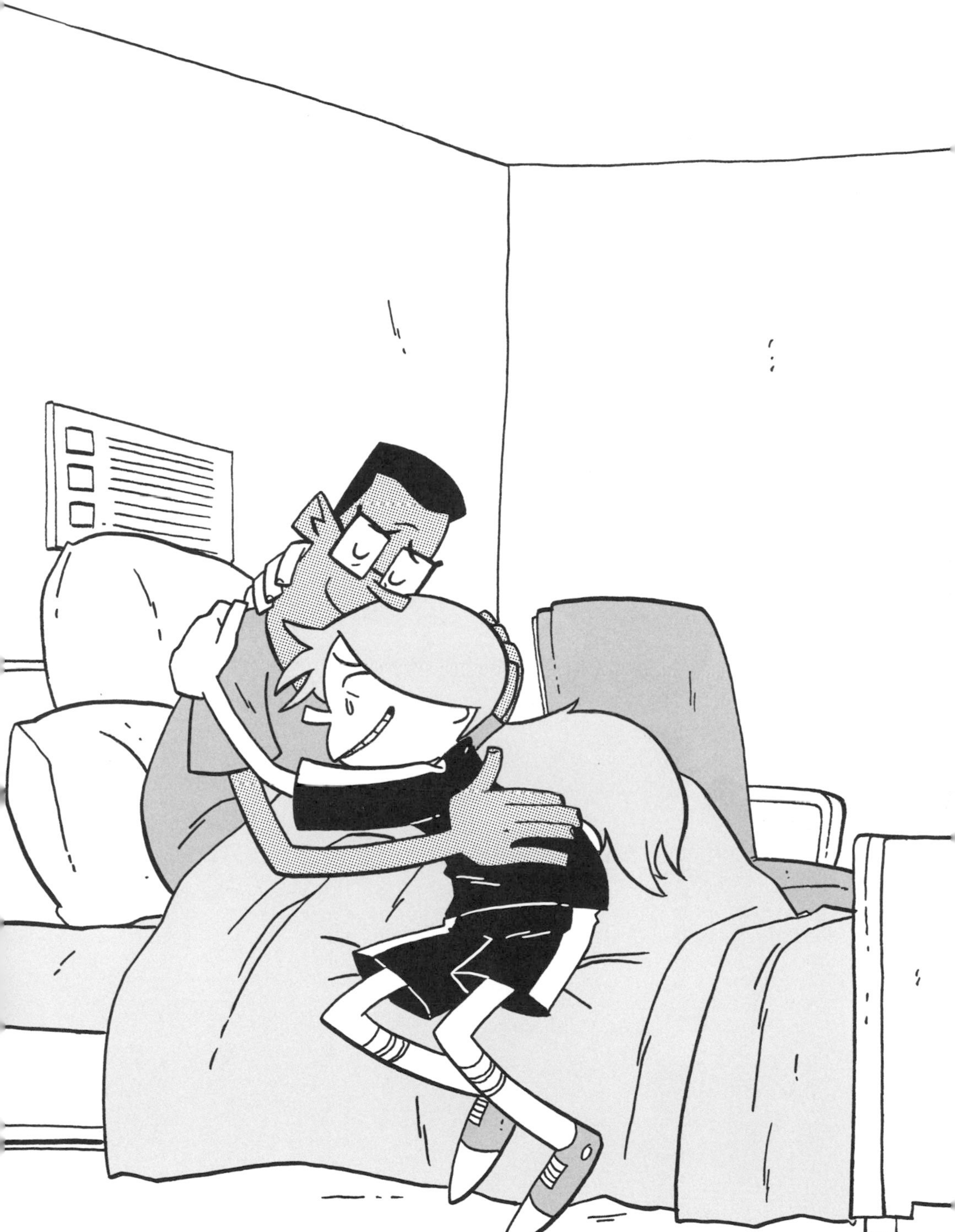

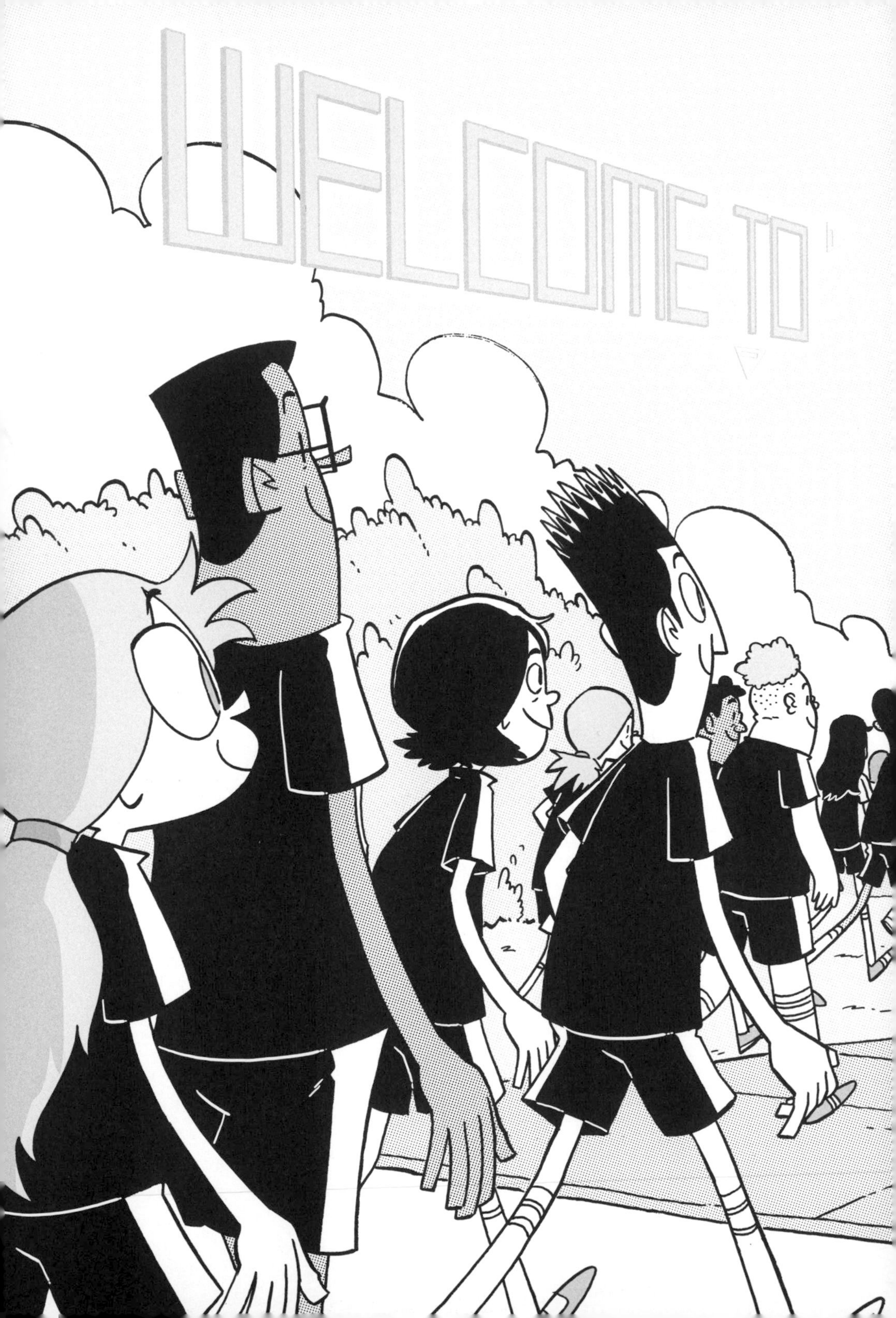
WELCOME TO

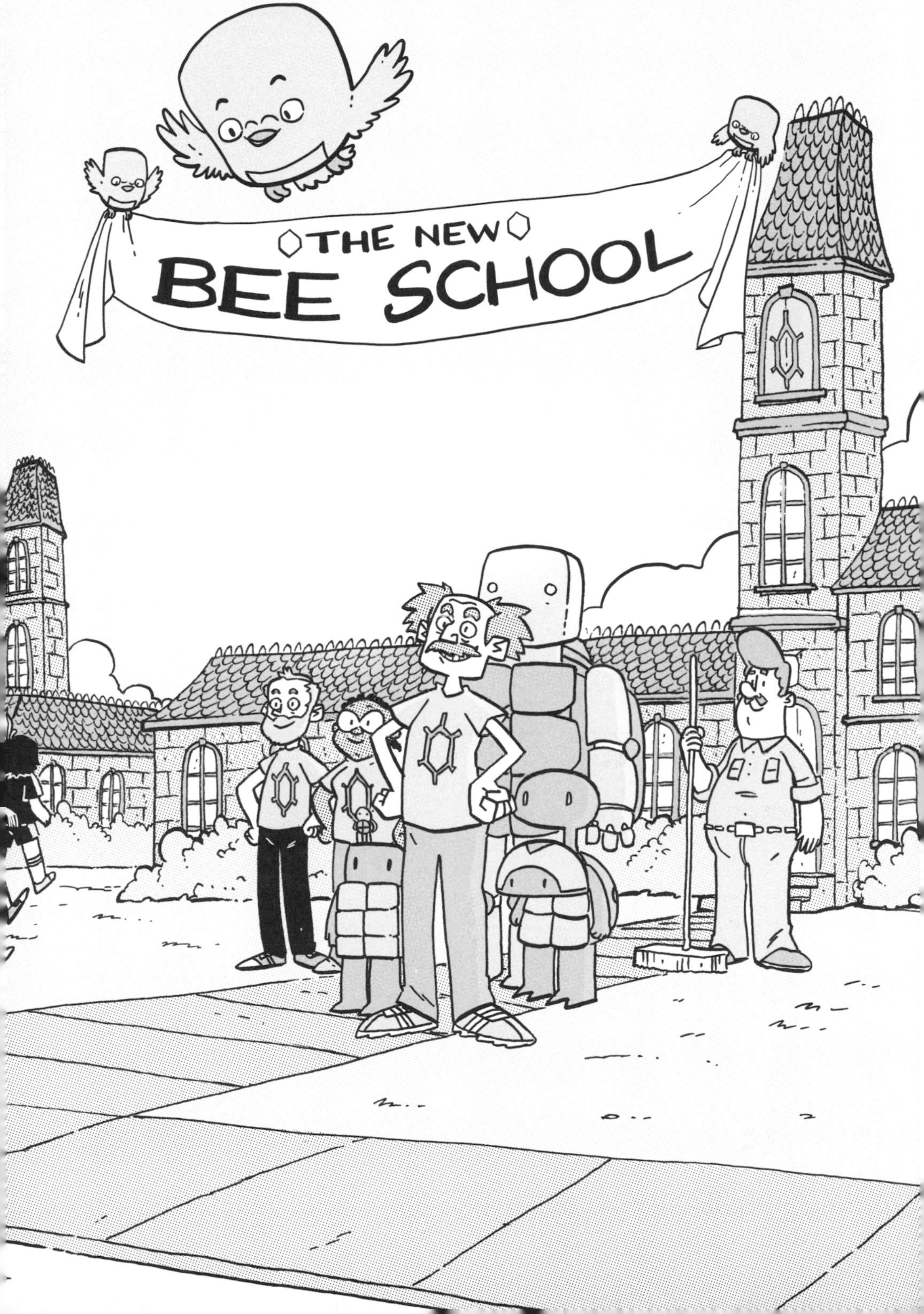
THE NEW
BEE SCHOOL

01010100
01001000
01000101
01000101
01001110
01000100

Ready to start coding?

Visit www.secret-coders.com

Check out these other books
in the Secret Coders series!

Secret Coders
Paths & Portals
Secrets & Sequences
Robots & Repeats
Potions & Parameters

The Making of Secret Coders

From the beginning, I knew Professor Bee would be a square. I don't mean somebody who's boring, I mean a shape with four equal, straight sides and four right angles. This character was inspired by *Flatland*, a science fiction classic first published in 1884. In that book, author Edwin Abbott firmly establishes his square-ness.

I decided to base the rest of my character designs on shapes too. It's hard to tell now, but Hopper's design started with circles. Eni is made up of rectangles and Josh triangles.

I sent my initial drawings to Mike, who added his own flair, making the Coders look a thousand times better.

PAGE 16.

Panel 1.

MOM: [1]
I've already talked to your grandparents. We're going to live with them for a while.

[2]
We'll have your father transferred to a nearby hospital.

HOPPER: [3]
Mom, please--

Panel 2.

MOM: [4]
I need you to understand something, Hopper.

Panel 3.

MOM: [5]
These past few days… I've never lived in so much _fear_ in all my life.

Panel 5.

HOPPER: [6]
Mom. Just one more day. _Please._

Panel 7.

MOM: [7]
Fine.

MOM: [8]
One more day.

This is how I wrote Secret Coders. I did rough drawings (called thumbnails) of every page. Next I typed up the script. Then I scanned in the drawings and inserted them into my script. I found this to be an efficient way to get the story across to Mike.

—Gene

Most comic book writers only provide a script. I'm incredibly fortunate to have Gene as a creative partner on Secret Coders—Gene is a writer *and* an artist. Gene's thumbnails offered a basic blueprint of the comic page, and I built on that.

I penciled digitally on a twenty-two inch Cintiq tablet. I laid out the panels first, then dropped in the text (dialogue, narration, etc.) so that I could account for how much room was left for the art. The art and the words need the right balance of space. Once that was done, I sketched out word balloons and blocked out the backgrounds and characters. Then I did another layer of pencils with more emphasis on detail, facial expressions, and movement.

At that point I'm usually ready for inks, since I like my pencils loose—it gives a more spontaneous feel to the art. I'll print out the digital pencils on smooth two-ply Bristol paper. For the characters or anything organic I inked with a fine-tipped Zebra brush pen. For backgrounds or anything with straight lines I used .02 to .05 Micron felt-tipped pens. Then I scanned the page at a high resolution and cleaned up the artwork in Photoshop.

You may wonder why I don't ink digitally as well, and the truth is, I like inking by hand! It's almost relaxing—I can sit on the couch, put on a couple movies, and before you know it, my work is done for the day.

—Mike

Mike: You're shockingly talented. Working with you to bring Secret Coders to life has been an amazing experience. Thank you.

My wife and kids: Thank you for inspiring me every day with your love, care, and goofiness.

First Second Books: Thanks for taking a chance on such a nerdy project. A cartoonist could not ask for a better home.

My agent Judy Hansen: Thanks for all your help with the tiny print.

Every one of our readers: You are the best. THE BEST. You reading our story is a tremendous, tremendous honor. Keep reading and keep coding!

—Gene

To Gene Luen Yang: A thousand thanks for taking me on as a partner in this enterprise and teaching me about coding along the way—and for being a pretty awesome guy. Good luck, Gene—maybe one day you'll enjoy some success in comics.

—Mike